THE COLD NIGHT

A JACKLYN STONE THRILLER

SUSAN SPECHT ORAM

SOS COMMUNICATIONS LLC

Published by SOS Communications LLC in 2025

www.susanspechtoram.com

First Edition

ISBN: 979-8-9926053-2-7 (paperback)

ISBN: 979-8-9926053-1-0 (e-book)

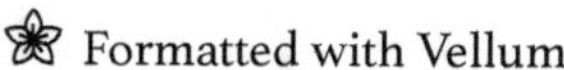 Formatted with Vellum

PREVIOUSLY

PREVIOUSLY IN:

SHORE LODGE

Jacklyn Stone, a grieving widow and garden store owner, is admitted by her greedy son to Shore Lodge, a secure psychiatric facility. She must escape to rescue her dog and reclaim her home.

BY MIDNIGHT

Jacklyn helps friends gather money to keep a debt collector at bay, but the clock is ticking in a race against time.

THE WINTER STORM

Jacklyn gathers friends and returns to Shore Lodge to

free four residents from a secure psychiatric unit. But a storm is brewing, and her son is out to thwart her every move.

1

IRENA

I stand trembling at the kitchen sink, terror coursing through my veins. My thirteen-year-old daughter is missing. Blinking back tears, I stab at my phone to put it on speaker mode and set it on the counter. Dusk is closing in on Christmas Eve, but my neighbors' flood lights illuminate a rare Pacific Northwest snowfall dusting lawns with a layer of white. Fat flakes drift down, and I stifle a sob.

Drawing a deep breath, I say to my friend Violet, who is on the other end of the line, "Kelly's not safe with my dad. He was sent to jail for killing a man, and he just got out. We've got to find her before he unleashes his hair-trigger temper on her."

Violet says in stern voice, "Read me the note he left."

I hurry to the kitchen table, stare at a note scrawled in

black marker and read aloud, "You didn't let me see Kelly, so I took her with me. Don't call the police. Dad.'

I burst into tears, shoulders shuddering, and as I blubber, Violet says, "What time did they leave your house?"

"I don't know. I left this morning and just got home."

"Call her and see if she picks up."

I stifle a sob. "I did, but her phone's in the kitchen. No teenage girl would leave their phone behind, so my dad must've made her do it. Where is she?"

"Don't worry, we'll find her. I'll look into this, and I'll call you back. Do you have video surveillance cameras outside your house?"

I put my head in my hands and moan. "I don't. Nothing bad happens in our small town, so I thought I didn't need them."

"Except it does," she says in a calm, clear voice. "It may look like Mayberry, but it isn't. Not when you look beneath the surface. I'd like you to take a deep breath, drink some water and sit down. Check her socials and think about where your dad might have taken her. Is there anywhere special he talked about going?"

I massage my throbbing temples and force myself to focus. "He talked about Canada sometimes when I was young, and he said he'd like to live in a fishing shack on a river in Alaska."

"Okay, that helps. Hang in there. We're on it, and I'll call if we find anything."

Hanging up, I grimace and scold myself. This is all my

fault for not staying home with my daughter today, on a holiday no less. What kind of mother abandons her daughter to take a day gallivanting across the water in a winter storm with friends. Not a good one, apparently.

Tears stream down my cheeks at how I've messed up the most important part of my life. Kelly is my everything, but now she's been abducted by her estranged grandfather who is prone to fits of rage. I knew that when I told my dad not to come around after he got out of prison and showed up at my house after years of silence. If I had been kinder to him, he might not have taken Kelly. This must be backlash for how I treated him, and his way of teaching me a lesson.

I wipe away tears with the back of my hand and blow my nose. My dad hasn't changed. A loving grandfather wouldn't take a thirteen-year-old girl away from home without her mother's permission. Revenge is his favorite meal, served with a side of seething hot anger at how my mom and I abandoned him and the world is against him.

Shaking my fist in the air, I say, "I'll find you, Dad, and I'll bring back my daughter."

JACKLYN

I nod and smile at the group gathered around my dining table, grateful to be with friends and family for Christmas Eve dinner. Outside, a snowstorm rages and wind batters the bungalow. The one-story home shudders, creaks and groans. I eye Del, who was a resident of Shore Lodge until this afternoon. He fled the facility and joined us on a boat trip from Cedar Island to Millersville. He picks at a red placemat.

I say, "How're you doing, Del? Leaving Shore Lodge is a lot to process, isn't it?"

He shrugs. "It's daunting, and I've never liked change, but I'll get over it."

I nod and consider all that has transpired since my husband Albert died almost a year ago. My grown kids talked me into taking a short stay at Shore Lodge that turned into a living nightmare behind locked doors in a secure psychiatric unit, and things went downhill from there.

Inhaling a slow, deep breath, I appreciate my daughter, sitting with my grandson at the table. She didn't realize what my son was up to, but Dusty deserves an acting award for how he tricked me and locked me away. He must have had it all planned out, because he was certainly efficient in dismantling my life and making off with my money in record time. I drum my fingers on the table, glad to be rid of him. He's not invited to this dinner, despite his being here every previous year, and there will be no unwanted guest named Dusty in my home tonight or ever.

My daughter Rose sets down her fork and says to Del, "I hate change too. It's tough to adjust and try new things."

My grandson Max says, "Not me, I want to ride a pony and drive a race car and go kayaking."

Rose shushes him. "That's enough. Let other people talk."

My best friend Mary glances at me and says, "Your grandmother and I had a tough time kayaking years ago. We got back to shore, and I sold my kayak the next day."

Mercury, my new friend who is a violin maker, tugs on his long gray beard. "It can be rough out there. Currents can be strong."

I bite my lower lip and recall how we fought the current carrying us away to Cypress Island. We dug in and paddled hard until our backs, shoulders and arms ached.

Clearing my throat, I say, "The Salish Sea offers both danger and delight, and you have to stay vigilant and hope you survive."

They cock their heads, looking concerned, so I add, "But enough of me prattling on. Let's clear the table and prepare for chocolate fondue, our Christmas Eve family tradition."

Max stands and frowns. "I wish Uncle Dusty was here." His eyes open wide, and he glances at me. "Let's call and invite him."

I go over and mess with his mop of brown hair before giving him a great big hug. "Sorry, bud, but it's not a good idea. I told Dusty not to darken my door after what he did to me, putting me in Shore Lodge."

Max sighs. "Okay."

My dog Buddy magically appears by my side, perhaps because I called my grandson Bud. I bend down and rub his soft beagle-mix ears. "Max, why don't you give Buddy a treat? And then play in the living room for a while?"

I take plates into the kitchen, and Max runs in and steps on a stool to reach the box of dog biscuits. Buddy sits, wagging his tail, watching Max's every move. They trot off together, and I go around patting each of my friends on the back, murmuring how glad I am that they're here. My hidden unsaid meaning is that I'm beyond grateful to be home and not locked up in Shore Lodge. Before my husband passed away, I never thought to appreciate the luxury of living with fresh air to breathe, room to roam and a to-do list of my own each day to accomplish.

Mercury flips his dish towel over his left shoulder and turns to me, opening his arms wide. I step into his arms, feeling the warmth from his body, and he whispers, "We should be celebrating your freedom tonight, don't you think?"

I nod, but a tear trickles down my cheek. "Yes, and the fact that I survived the tempest with my troubled son."

Mary shelves plates. "And that you and your crew made it back to town today, navigating through a storm."

I shake my head. "Nurse Wright and the administrator at Shore Lodge were livid that Del left. They seemed desperate. Maybe they lost residents after I escaped?"

Del holds up his soapy hands at the sink. "That's what I heard. A few residents were pulled out by family and moved elsewhere. But nowhere is perfect, so I'm not sure what they found was an improvement." He points a finger at me. "As you know, the second floor is secure compared to the first, where I was. After you got out, they welded the second-floor windows in place, so no one will escape again."

A shiver runs up my spine, and I shudder. "That makes me lucky to be on this side of the channel." A horrible idea flits through my head. If something happened to me and I was admitted to Shore Lodge a second time, I don't think I'd survive being with Nurse

Wright's wrath behind locked doors without fresh briny air blowing in from the water.

I squint at Rose, Mercury, Del, Mary and Fred, giving them a good hard look. "Promise me that no matter what happens in the future, even if my mind turns to mush many years down the road, that you will not take me to Shore Lodge. Nurse Wright has a vendetta against me and made my life miserable."

Rose says, "Why did she dislike you so much?"

"She wants her residents to follow rules and be docile. Does that sound like me?"

They laugh, and Rose reaches out, wrapping her arms around me. She whispers in my ear. "I'm glad you made it home, Mom, and I'm sorry for my part in Dusty's plan. I can understand why you didn't invite him to dinner tonight."

I step back. "No need to keep apologizing. You were busy."

She turns to help wash the dishes and clean the kitchen, and I carry our orange fondue pot out to the dining room. As I plug it in, I reflect that I'll never grow tired of hearing Rose apologize for her part in my being in a secure psych unit, and I'll never completely understand how she ignored what Dusty was doing after her dad died.

I pour one cup of heavy cream, a pinch of salt and dark chocolate chips into the pot and sniff the air. My mouth waters, imagining eating a bite of bread coated in melted chocolate.

Mary brings out baskets with chunks of bread and sets them on the table. She pats my back. "Nothing like the smell of chocolate to soothe the soul, eh?"

I smiled. "This and a cup of coffee are two of the best things in life."

She glances around and waves a hand over the pot, sniffing the air. "No cinnamon this year? Or chili pepper?"

I make a face. "That was a failed experiment, at least with Max. No, we'll stick with the plain version for broad appeal." Rose and Max carry out plates with sliced apples and bananas. I give them a sly look and say, "But I suppose we could try dipping dried figs and broccoli and Brussel sprouts in the fondue. What do you think of that, Max?"

Rose sets out fondue forks and shoots me a smile.

He furrows his brow. "If I have to, I guess I'll try it, but I'd rather not."

"I'm just kidding. Vegetables and chocolate don't belong together in my book." Stirring the melting chocolate mixture, memories of the many times my husband and I sat with the kids in this room for Christmas Eve fondue swim before my eyes. I dab my eyes with a tissue and call to the others, "Come to the table for a special treat."

Everyone slides into their seats, and Max grins. We're about to pick up our fondue forks and perform our ritual of clanking them together when a sound outside makes us stop mid-air. I cock my head and my heart thuds. A truck out front backfires.

My muscles tense, and I rest a hand on my suddenly sour stomach. I hope I'm wrong, but my best guess is the sound of a truck backfiring means my errant son who was not invited has arrived.

I lock eyes with Rose, because I don't want her brother to stop by, not tonight or any night, not after what he did. Dusty admitted me to a secure psychiatric facility and spent my money. Treating me as a money bag for his own gain meant I wrote him out of my will, but I haven't bothered to tell him that yet. The less he knows about my private affairs, the better.

I jump up and peek out the window at what looks like my son's truck parked out front. Mercury grips the table edge. "Whatever happens, we'll deal with it together. You're not alone in this."

Mary's voice wavers when she says, "Do you think Dusty would have the nerve to come here after what he did to you?"

Fred runs a hand through his thinning brown hair. "I'd put my money on him showing up and doling out satchels of resentment."

Mary nods. "He won't hurt you with the rest of us backing you up."

I cross my arms. "Stinkweed should be his middle name. Or skunk cabbage."

A chuckle ripples through the room, but we're all on edge, listening and waiting for what will happen next.

Heavy footsteps approach the front door, and my chest

tightens. Someone knocks once with a hard fist, and the door rattles in the frame.

My pulse races, and I rush over to make sure the door is locked, the way I left it. My palms turn cold. The metal door knob starts to turn.

I flick the lock closed, but it's too late, and the door opens. I put a foot in front of it, but a mightier force than mine shoves it open.

I turn to my friends and family. "I locked the door. Who left it unlocked?"

Max pops out of his chair and comes over. "I did, when I went out with Buddy."

My dog trots over, sniffing at the door.

Dusty steps inside, standing tall, dripping wet and windblown with red cheeks. "Hello, Mother. Merry Christmas, everyone."

The wind howls, blowing in bits of snow with his unwelcome entrance. Goosebumps prick my arms, and I tell myself not to fear my own flesh and blood. In a firm voice, I say, "I told you not to come here unless you were invited."

Dusty ignores me and slides into Max's vacant seat. "I'm hungry. How about some dinner, Mom, dear?"

3

VIOLET

I hang up from talking with Irena about Kelly being taken and turn to my sister, Karina. She and Bernard Frackus, her grandmother's secret boyfriend, are spreading a red tablecloth on the kitchen table in Gigi's Café for our Christmas Eve dinner. Karina adds two pewter candlesticks, and Bernard lights the candles. The old creaking two-story house smells like family, good food and friendship.

I clear my throat and unfurl my clenched fists. They won't be happy to hear what I'm about to say. "I'm sorry. I was really looking forward to dinner, but I have to head to the office."

Karina bites her lower lip. "But dinner's almost ready. What's going on?"

Bernard fiddles with his black-framed glasses and frowns. "Maybe we can help."

Crossing my arms, I tap a toe because I've got to get going, right now. Every minute matters in finding an abducted child. "Kelly was taken by her grandfather, who just got out of prison and showed up in town. He left a note saying he took her and not to call the police. I need to move fast and track them down before they cross over into Canada and disappear forever."

Karina slaps a hand over her open mouth. "Oh no, she's only thirteen."

I grab my purse, sling it over my shoulder and move toward the back door. "I wish I could stay and enjoy our meal, but I've got to get on this right away. You two stay and eat.

Bernard cocks his head. "But he's her grandfather, so it must be okay? He's family, after all." He picks up a blue pottery bowl with garlic mashed potatoes and a pat of butter melting in the middle, setting it on the table.

My heart thuds, and I sniff the air, inhaling the mouth-watering aroma of garlic and butter. Normally, I'd be out of here in seconds, but I only recently connected with my half-sister and I care about keeping a positive relationship. I slap my hand on the doorframe and blow out a breath. "Irena says Kelly's not safe with him. He killed a man in Eastern Washington and was sent to prison for it. This is not a kind, gentle grandfather taking Kelly for a holiday ride. This is an angry, bitter man who might hurt or kill her in retaliation for Irena telling him to stay away from them."

Karina's eyes open wide, and she pulls off her apron, tossing it on the kitchen counter. "We'll go with you."

He nods. "We'll help. We'll sharpen pencils and do whatever you need. Let's get Kelly back."

I resist the urge to roll my eyes and doubt two civilians can assist in a case like this.

My sister says, "We'll pack up the food to take with us and eat while we work."

He clenches his jaw, gazing at me.

I open my hands. "Sure, why not? But let's get out of here. The sooner we find Kelly, the better."

Karina is a pro at packing up food orders to go because she runs a café when she isn't painting canvasses and making pottery. In less than five minutes, we're out the door and headed to my company, Outrigger Services. My car smells like chicken stroganoff and garlic mashed potatoes.

Bernard leans forward in the back seat. "How well does Kelly know her grandfather?"

I drive down the block and turn right. "They just met when he came to town recently. Irena told him not to come back because of what he did when she was young."

Karina, riding shotgun, purses her lips. "Poor Kelly. That's rough."

I turn left and pull over, parking outside my office. We step out of the car into howling wind barreling down the street. Wreaths hung from light poles sway and creak as the metal groans. A stack of beer kegs by a brew pub are lit up with colorful lights. But no one else is around downtown on this cold night.

Reaching into the car for a box with part of our Christmas Eve dinner, I blink as snowflakes fly into my eyes. "It'd be scary for her, to be taken by a grandfather she only just met. We've got to move fast."

Karina grabs a plastic container. "I hope she won't miss Christmas with Irena."

Bernard picks up a brown paper bag, and I hip bump the door shut, clicking my key fob to lock it. Ours is a small town, and no one is around, but I won't tempt fate and leave it unlocked. In a tense voice, I say, "Okay, let's go."

I open the lower entry door, and Karina and I hurry up steps to my office on the second floor. Bernard climbs the stairs behind us.

"We'll get her back," Karina says in an upbeat tone of voice that makes me appreciate her all the more. In cases like this, you must move quickly. We'll be nimble, stay alert for signs of her granddad and extract her without harm, I hope.

He leans against the railing. "I have every confidence in you, Violet."

"Thanks, I hope I deserve it and this goes well."

I set down the box, unlock the office and hope we'll find Kelly, bringing her home soon.

4

IRENA

I gulp down a glass of water and glance outside as snowflakes fly past. The temperature is dropping, and snow is starting to accumulate on the ground. I swallow hard, because if Kelly were here, she'd run outside and play, making snow angels. Gnawing on a fingernail, I make a vow to find my daughter. Violet is trying to locate her, but I must do all I can to bring her back.

I tense my jaw, recalling when my mother and I moved to this small waterfront town in Washington State. When my father was sent to prison on the east side of the mountains when I was young, Mom and I headed west and never told him where we went. He recently showed up in Millersville, but I refused to have anything to do with him. I won't forgive him for how he treated my mother. Tears stream down my cheeks, and I hope my daughter will tap her strength and smarts to protect herself from his wrath.

Pacing the kitchen with my hands behind my back, I mull over who else might help me find Kelly. A tentative smile spreads across my face, and I grab my phone, texting Violet that I'll contact Special Agent McNalley, an FBI agent I met when my ex-husband was in trouble. Checking the time, I see it's six in the evening on Christmas Eve and with each passing minute, Kelly is farther away from home.

My pulse picks up, and I wipe my moist palms on my jeans. I have to save my daughter before she disappears forever into wild parts of Alaska or wherever Dad is planning to take her.

Knocking on a wood table for luck, I dial the FBI agent's number.

A woman answers. "Special Agent McNalley, how can I help you?"

5

DUSTY

I settle into a chair, glance around the dining table and smile, looking each person in the eye. My goal in coming here was to eat a good meal and celebrate the holiday without being alone, like I've been. Maybe there's a chance my mother might warm up to me, so I can take my construction company back. Mom's friends, my sister and my nephew let their fondue forks fall to the table with a clatter. It looks like they're about to eat dessert.

"Any dinner left?"

My sister stares at me for a moment. "I'll fix you a plate."

I could get it myself and grab some grub in the kitchen, but I want to stay in the dining room holding court and maintaining control over this motley group. Mom is standing and crossing her arms, tapping a toe and looking ticked off. The frown on her face is definitely not becoming.

While the others fiddle with their fondue forks or stare at the tablecloth, my mom's new friend Mercury holds my gaze. I stare right back, not blinking or backing off, until he shakes his head and glances away. In the kitchen, Buddy laps water from a bowl.

Fred runs a hand through his thinning hair. "Didn't you hear your mother? You're not welcome here after what you did."

I shrug my shoulders. "I'm glad I got here before you ate dessert. Fondue was my favorite part of Christmas Eve dinner growing up, until a certain fondue fork incident occurred."

Rose sets a plate of food down before me, and I nod to her. "Thanks."

Max nudges me. "I picked out the chicken."

I clap him on the back. "Good job, my man."

Mercury adjusts a polka dot bow tie attached to his long gray beard. He leans his elbows on the table. "Okay, I'll bite. What happened with the unfortunate fondue fork situation?"

Rose glances nervously at me, shaking her head. "Not in front of Max."

I chomp down on a chicken leg, chew for a bit and swallow. "It happened this way." Crumbs and flecks of food fly from my lips.

Mary makes a face, Fred cringes, and Mom puts her

hands on her hips, glaring at me. By drawing out the story and making myself at home, I'll show them who holds the power in this house tonight. I'll create a crack of uncertainty among folks here about Mom's mental acuity and plant seeds of doubt that I'll reap later, making the dinner a success.

Holiday tunes play in the background, and the house smells like Christmas, with scented candles and cedar boughs covering the mantle. I shovel in a bite of macaroni salad and smack my lips. "It happened this way and in this very room. On Christmas Eve when we were kids, Mom and Dad were in the kitchen, and Rose and I set the table for dessert with fondue forks. I may or may not have taunted her, but that was nothing compared to what happened next."

Rose drums her fingers on the table. "Dusty, don't. Just stop."

Max pokes my arm. "What happened?"

Mom says, "Dusty, finish your meal and go home. Tonight is about having a fun, celebratory dinner, but this has become contentious, with you dredging up the past."

I gulp down a chunk of crispy chicken and wipe my hands on my jeans. Buddy trots out from the kitchen and sniffs my fingers, but I lean forward, putting my elbows on the table. "Am I making you uncomfortable by revealing family secrets, bringing them to light? Don't hide your sins in a dark closet."

Mom glowers. "It's not me that needs to be forgiven. You'd better get out a mirror and look at it long and hard."

I chuckle. "I do, every day, but I'm not sure if you follow your own advice. This is your favorite holiday, so where's your Christmas spirit? It's a time for friends and family to gather together, and that's why I'm here, to mend broken fences because Dad isn't here to smooth things over and help us get along."

Mom grabs the back of a chair and doubles over, breathing hard.

I clear my throat. "What happened that night long ago is Rose stabbed me with a fondue fork. I've still got the mark on my cheek, from where it hung when I ran out to the kitchen. And when I told my mother, what did she say?"

Mom glares. "Dusty, this isn't the time to air our differences."

I shake my head. "If it was up to you, there'd never be a good time."

Rose frowns. "Let's talk about something else."

I sit back, and Buddy noses me, licking my hand, but I pull away, pointing a calloused finger at those gathered around the table, stopping at each person before moving on. An older guy with big ears from Shore Lodge shudders and averts his eyes, tugging on an ear lobe. I guess we know who's the chicken in this group. What a wimp.

"None of you know my mother as well as you think you do, and because you're close to her, I'll let you in on a secret. She still has issues with her memory, and she's not in touch with reality. She's fooling you. Like when I told her Rose stuck me with the fondue fork, which was dangling from my cheek, she brushed it off and said I deserved it. I mean, who does that? Her son was injured by his sibling, but she shrugged it off."

The older guy from Shore Lodge whistles. "That's some story. You should tell it to a therapist or share it in group counselling."

I shrug off his remark. "What I need is money, not counselling. I don't need therapy. I know how to help myself."

Mom narrows her eyes. "You'd help yourself by taking my money, but that's over. You've seen the last dime from me."

Max leans over, breath hot in my ear. "Do you still have the mark? Let me see."

I tap my right cheek. "It dangled right there and hurt for weeks, not just on my cheek but deep in my soul. That's what started me writing poetry to explore my feelings about being the unappreciated, unseen child."

Mom says, "This is outrageous. We bent over backwards to help you. Now you come here on a holiday, Christmas Eve no less, and accuse me of being a bad parent? We don't air family problems ever, especially in front of guests."

She marches to the door and holds it open. "Goodbye,

Dusty. You know the way out. Happy holidays and don't come back unless I invite you."

Cold air blows inside, and I stand, brushing crumbs off my flannel shirt. "Would a reasonable person ignore a son who was injured? She didn't take me to a doctor or the emergency room. The wound became infected, and I had to take an antibiotic. And that's only one instance among many I could share with you."

Fred says, "I think we've heard enough."

Mercury tugs on his mustache. "You need help, dragging this around from the past. Go get counselling."

Rose nods. "Move on. It all happened years ago."

The guy with big ears squirms in his seat. "I did that, and it helped. You ought to give it a try."

I lean over the table, looking at each person. "I ask you this, who in their right mind would take over a construction company when they know nothing about building? No one would, unless they had delusions of grandeur. I urge you to take a step back and observe my mother for signs of memory loss. She's putting on an act, and I contend she's not right in her head. Now that we have that sorted, who is ready for dessert?"

Jaws drop. Mom's friends swallow.

Rose bangs her hand on the table. "She's fine. There's nothing wrong with Mom."

I stomp to the door, brush past Mom and slam it shut. Turning to the table, I stretch out my arms and grin. "I don't know about you, but I'd like some of my mother's fabulous chocolate fondue. What do you say? Shall we get this party started?"

They sit dull-eyed, looking down.

I go over and pound a fist on the table, so dishes rattle. "What did I just say? Let's get dessert going. That's what Christmas Eve is all about, isn't it? Celebrating the holiday with friends and family."

They glance at each other and slowly stand.

I smack a fist into my palm. "Let's move. Get going. I'm getting impatient, and you don't want that to happen. I'm already in a bad mood because I wasn't invited to your party."

Putting my hands on my hips, I glare at my mother. "Wouldn't any sane person invite their son to a family and friends dinner at her home?"

They scurry in a cluster out to the kitchen, as if there's safety in numbers, making me chuckle and reminding me of hurrying hens chased by a wolf. I'm the big bad wolf, and I've come to consume whatever I want. Merry Christmas, Mom, I'll help myself to your hidden treats and treasures. I deserve that, and Dad would back me one-hundred percent.

6

MARY

Dusty stomps to the bathroom, and I blow out a breath, my shoulders relaxing, but bracing myself for the next round of his toxic blend of verbal abuse and venom. I lock eyes with my husband, because this is not the festive evening we expected. Instead, we're witnesses to a family feud that feels ugly and way too personal to be voiced at a holiday dinner with friends. We sit at the table, stunned into silence by Dusty taking up all the air in the room since he arrived. Being uninvited hasn't stopped him one bit.

Bittersweet chocolate mixed with milk melts in a fondue pot, giving off a mouth-watering aroma. Serving trays hold strawberries and sliced bananas, ready to be dipped into creamy chocolate. Jacklyn adds a splash of vanilla extract. As she stirs, I lean over to her and say in a low voice, "You always make Christmas Eve special. And I know you. You were a good mother, so don't doubt yourself for even a minute. End of story."

She beams. "Thanks, I appreciate that."

Mercury says something, and she turns toward him. My husband whispers to me, "Let's make our excuses and go."

I speak softly in his ear. "We can't leave now with Dusty here. He's so angry."

Fred nods. "Fine, we'll stay. But he could be right. Maybe her cognitive skills are impaired."

I narrow my eyes. "We'll talk about this later. She's my best friend, and I won't have you doubting her sanity."

Fred shrugs. "Running a construction company would be challenging for anyone, let alone someone coming back from the precipice of grief."

Dusty clomps into the dining room and glowers. "What're you two talking about? Share it with the rest of us."

I say, "We were talking about going home early to watch a Christmas movie in bed, but we decided to stay and celebrate the holiday with all of you."

Dusty belches and rubs his belly. "Let's get on with the fondue."

I scold myself for being a coward and screw up my courage. "You know what? You are being verbally abusive to your wonderful mother, and the rest of us don't appreciate that. You need to be nicer to her. She's your mother, for heaven's sake."

He hums a tune and brushes lint from his shoulder.

Jacklyn holds up an index finger. "I'd like to clear something up and point out that I'm agile and alert and there's nothing wrong with my mind. I hope you don't doubt that, because of what Dusty said."

Dusty sighs. "Let's table that discussion for the time being, because I have more to say on that topic, and move on to dessert. But I have to ask, would someone with mental acuity make a plea for sanity? They wouldn't have to, would they? It'd be self-evident, and we'd know she was sharp and of sound mind."

He grabs a fondue fork and thrust it up in the air. "Rose, which cheek would you like to stab this time? The right or the left? I can live with either one, if it makes you feel better. You've got a demanding job and a busy life. Go ahead, take out some of your frustrations on me, Mom won't stop you. She doesn't care about me."

Jacklyn clenches a fist. "Stop this nonsense and get out. You're making a scene. We were having a great time until you arrived. You're ruining the evening for all of us."

Max grabs his mother. "Don't hurt him."

Rose says, "Your uncle's kidding, but I wish he'd stop." She stares at her brother.

Dusty holds up his hands. "She's right, and I'm sorry if I frightened you, bud. Just a little sibling humor to lighten the mood and create levity on the eve of a happy holiday."

I glance at Jacklyn and roll my eyes. Dusty has brought anger and angst to the table. He's carrying a heavy burden of resentment that could burst into flames at any moment.

Dusty jabs an index finger at me, and we lock eyes. My heart skips a beat, but I'm not backing down. My friend deserves our support, especially after what her husband did before he died, hiding financial secrets.

"I see you rolling your eyes, Mary," he says in a low, rumbling voice, "and I don't appreciate your disrespect. At the very least, keep negative comments and your bad attitude to yourself until you're out the door on your way home."

"Be careful, Dusty," Fred says. "You're on thin ice."

I tap a finger on the table and count the minutes until Fred and I can leave without hurting Jacklyn's feelings. The sooner we've eaten fondue and we're out the door with our coats on, the better, but I can't leave my friend Jacklyn alone with Dusty.

"You sound so angry," I say to him. "Your grief could be making you act this way. I know your father wouldn't have wanted you to carry this burden of grieving for so long."

He glowers. "What'd you mean?"

"Maybe you haven't allowed yourself to grieve your dad's death. I know I was angry and irritated when my mother passed away."

He taps a calloused finger to his lips. "I don't think that

fits my situation. I've been upfront about being sad since Dad died. And I've even written poems about it. I'm not hiding or suppressing it. But maybe my mother or my sister are."

Wooden chairs creak, and people squirm. My throat is dry, and I sip my Manhattan. I stand on wobbly legs, eager to escape the gloom in the room from Dusty's dark mood, which is penetrating every conversation and permeating each molecule we breathe. He brought a stink of resentment to the dinner table, and one of us must step up and confront him. "I think I'll refresh my drink. Anyone else?"

Fred, Mercury and Del rise and say in unison, "Good idea."

Jacklyn makes a sour face. "Come back quick, because the chocolate's melted. And keep your fondue forks to yourselves. We don't want to hear more stories about stabbing forks."

A strained chuckle ripples around the room. I'm Jacklyn's best friend, and this is the first I've heard of The Famous Fondue Fork Incident, where her son was stabbed. We're trapped with a madman masquerading as a grown man, harboring an angry child hidden inside. But before long, dessert will be consumed and the occasion will come to a close, and we'll run for home. This is the dinner party that turned into an awful event, where one person dominated the conversation and bullied the rest of us. I don't like it one bit. I've got to gather the courage to speak up and say my truth to Dusty, the one who is working us like a puppeteer and controlling our conversations.

In the kitchen, I pour a drink and blame myself for being passive. Speak up. Stop this madness. Do the right thing for your best friend.

7

DUSTY

My plan for ruining Mom's holiday party is coming together. I've planted seeds of doubt about her mental acuity, and I need to hammer home the message about her questionable memory. I scarf down a chunk of chocolate-coated bread, wipe my lips on a napkin and swig my Manhattan, setting the glass down with a thud.

Leaning back in the chair, I speak in a loud voice to interrupt ongoing conversations. "Now that I live near the mountains, I'm considering starting a mountaineering company. I'll charge a hefty fee per person to guide people up Pacific Northwest mountains, and they'll pay a premium for my concierge service."

Mom tilts her head. "This is the first I've heard of it, but it sounds like a good idea to start something new."

I dig in my jeans pocket and pull out a folded piece of

paper. "Did you forget? We talked about this over a month ago. I was going to call it Northwest Endeavors, but you pointed out that name was already taken, after you searched for it online. So, I settled on the name Pacific Northwest Endeavors."

Her face turns red, and she frowns. "I don't recall us discussing that."

"We did, but you've had a lot going on." I pocket the piece of paper before anyone asks to read it.

Mercury wipes chocolate from his lips with a napkin. "How many mountains you have summitted?"

I cock my head. "It's not the final destination that matters, it's the journey, right, Mom? Dad said life is like a river, taking twists and turns, and we need to learn to go with the flow."

Mom dabs at the corners of her eyes and stands. "I need some air. Be right back."

Mercury and Rose stand and say at the same time, "I'll go with you."

Mom shakes her head. "Thanks, but I need to be alone for a bit."

Rose says, "Take your coat, it's cold out."

When Mom flings open the door, snow and cold air rush inside. "I'll be fine, just like I always am. Don't worry about me, go on with your dessert."

The door closes, and a heavy silence settles over the table. No one will meet my gaze. The older guy with big ears squirms and pulls at his collar. "Is anyone else feeling hot in here? Maybe it's because they kept the temperature low at Shore Lodge. They said it was good for brain function."

I snap my attention to the man. "You were at Shore Lodge? What's your name?"

He swallows, and his Adam's apple bobs up and down. "I don't feel like telling you. It's no one's business but mine, and it's a privacy issue."

I slowly smile. "You were on Irena's boat, coming from Cedar Island this afternoon. Did my mother help you leave Shore Lodge? Nurse Wright and Dr. Henderson will want to know about this."

I pull out my phone to call Nurse Wright, but Fred thumps the table with a fist, and fondue forks rattle. The group gasps, but I chuckle, because I love making a scene and being the center of attention.

Fred's face is flushed. "Stop this at once. Leave the man alone and respect his privacy. Can't we just eat dessert in peace? You've already disturbed your mother by bringing up your father."

His eyes bore into mine, but I shrug and say, "No one's talked about Dad since he died, like he became invisible after his fatal heart attack. It's my job to rip back the curtain and remember him, to talk about him, even though the rest of you would rather forget he ever existed."

I glare at my sister for good measure. She says, "We all loved Dad and remember him in different ways. But some of us don't need to talk about him as often as you do."

I fiddle with my fondue fork and eye the creamy pot of chocolate on the table. I'd love to rip off the tablecloth, dump everything on the floor and splatter chocolate on the dining room walls, but I won't. I mustn't lose control because what matters is my end game, which is getting my construction company back.

Max looks down at the floor. "I miss Grandpops."

Rose pats his back. "Me too."

The front door opens, and Buddy bounds inside, shaking off snow and rolling around on the living room rug. Mom enters and closes the door. She gives me a steely-eyed gaze before bending and petting Buddy. "Good dog."

She joins us at the table, sliding into her seat and appearing calm. I regret needling her, because she has a steel core inside, as Dad used to say, and now she looks tough and ready to fight.

Mom reaches over, takes an apple slice and dips it in melted chocolate in the fondue pot. She chews and wipes her mouth on a napkin, saying, "Let's let worries and resentments fade and get back into the holiday spirit. I'd like all to be right with the world on Christmas Eve." She eyes me. "We can set aside our differences for tonight, can't we?"

My face heats, and I nod, feeling chastised like a child. I'm suddenly small and ten years old at the table. I clench my fists and stand. Clearing my throat, I say, "I think I'll turn in for the night. See you tomorrow."

Rose says, "I'm staying in your old room, and you need to help with the dishes."

"I thought you were going home," Mom says.

I stride over to the window, part the curtains and stare out at white snow blanketing the road and lawn. "It's not safe to drive right now. Maybe tomorrow after Millersville's one snow plow gets around town."

The guy with big ears says, "Only one snow plow? Surely they have more than that. What kind of place is this?"

Mercury smile, tugging on his mustache. "We're in a little town in the middle of nowhere, tucked away from big city troubles."

Mary says, "And the best place to live."

I shrug. "I'd leave, if my tires weren't bald. I planned on buying new ones, but I'm broke."

"Sounds rough," the big-eared man says.

Under his breath, Fred says, "Cry me a river."

My sister rolls her eyes. "That's a familiar tune."

Mom says, "Let's start on a new track and leave the past behind for tonight."

Mercury raises his glass. "Let's toast to that."

Mary smiles. "I agree."

I rub my right cheek. I'll mix with the group and drop little mentions of issues with Mom's memory, undermining their confidence in her, one grain of sand at a time. "I was going to go in my room and write a poem, but I guess I could celebrate Christmas, like we used to, with a toast at midnight."

Max flings open the front door and runs out, followed by Buddy, who yips and barks. "Snow!"

Rose calls to Max, "Take your coat and close the door."

But my nephew is long gone, and the snow is coming down hard, accumulating in deep drifts.

While the others clear the table, Mom and I stay in the dining room. She unplugs the fondue pot, stares at me with cold blue eyes and says in a low voice, "I know what you're trying to do, but it won't work. I'm on to you."

8

JACKLYN

I stand on the front porch, shivering in the freezing cold, and frown at a thick blanket of snow covering my yard and the quiet street. More than a foot of snow rests on the roof of my son's truck, and more is coming down. Crossing my arms, a stiff breeze blows past my cheeks and snowflakes fly into my eyes.

I blink and mutter to myself. I can't let Dusty mess with my mind. I can do this. I've come through worse.

With a howling wind whipping at my back, I turn to the door, rest my hand on the cold metal knob and let out a long sigh. The sooner the town's snow plow arrives, the better for all concerned. I step inside, close the door and join the others at the table. We're a silent bunch, dipping strawberries and bananas into melted chocolate. Inhaling the aroma of melted chocolate, I half-smile. No matter what happens, I can survive being under one roof with this boy I birthed, even though I'd like him to high-tail it out of here right now.

Max says, "This is the best part of Christmas, besides the gifts."

"That's right," Dusty says, and I grit my teeth for what my flesh and blood nemesis will say next. He clears his throat and sends a sharp look my way, adding, "And that's why we're gathered here tonight. To celebrate the holiday and our mutual support system, grown out of our common bond of living in a small town. We're also cele-brating more light and longer days, and I'm looking forward to not getting up in the dark. The cabin I'm renting in Foothills is a dank little place compared to this. Maybe I should move back home. What do you think, Mom?"

I shake my head. "Not while I'm alive, and not after that. Isn't that right, Mary?"

Mary flashes a smile and gives me a thumbs up.

Dusty wipes his mouth with the tablecloth. "Speaking of Shore Lodge, shouldn't you both be back there? I'm sure they're missing you, Mom. And Del, I could make one phone call to Nurse Wright and have you hauled away from this house."

Del flinches, tossing his napkin down. His hands clench. "That's my business, so stay out of it. I don't tell anyone about my private life."

I jump to my feet and lean across the table, jabbing a finger at my son. "Stop taunting him. You're just trying to act like a big man, which makes you look a small boy. Shame on you for poking and prodding at someone's personal problems." I stand back and rest my hands on my hips. "All I've got to say is, back off, buster, or else."

Dusty chuckles and opens his hands. "Or else what? I bet Nurse Wright would like to know where you are, Mom, and Dr. Henderson could have another look at you. I have her private cell number. Maybe I'll call her right now."

I march over and snatch my son's phone, shoving it in my back pocket. My pulse races at memories of my time at Shore Lodge. "I've had enough of that talk and your threats. Don't be rude to my guests."

He frowns, swinging his arms at me. "Give it back."

I step away and stride around the table. "I'll give it to you when you leave. Now behave. While you're here, I expect you to be kind and courteous."

He tips his head back and laughs. "Yammer, yammer. You're all talk and no action." He raises his voice, mimicking me. 'Be kind and courteous. Behave.'" He thumps a hand on the table. "I'm not a child, Mother dear. I'm a grown man."

"Then act like one."

"Now, now," Fred says. "Can we all settle down? This was supposed to be a nice dinner party, not a boxing match. Let's keep it civil."

Mary says, "That's right."

Mercury gives Rose a side glance. "Is this typical of

how Christmas Eve is for your family? Just a dull, boring dinner would be fine with me."

Rose sighs. "After my father died, everything changed."

I clutch the fondue pot and carry it to the kitchen, going past Dusty on the way. He's trying to cut me down, one stroke at a time. For a flicker of a second, I picture myself dumping chocolate on his deluded head to retaliate for him spinning lies about my memory. His mentioning his dad was surely meant to wound me, because he knows we're approaching my wedding anniversary, which is when my husband died. What a long, trying year it has been. When I have time, I'll think about how I'd like to honor Albert's passing.

Blinking back tears, I set the fondue pot on the counter. Mary comes in, putting fondue forks in the sink with a clatter, and she turns to me. "Anything I can do to help?"

I shake my head. "Thanks, but no. I'll get through this on my own."

She peers into my eyes. "We're here to help. You're not alone. Remember that."

Dusty comes in the kitchen carrying a stack of small dessert plates with gold rims that I picked up at a second-hand store. The air almost vibrates with anger. A vein throbs in his temple. His jaw is clenched, and his face is flushed. "Want these in the dishwasher?"

I'm determined to get through his short visit and remain civil, so I say, "In the sink will be fine."

Mercury pulls an apron over his head and starts washing dishes. Fred dries them.

I owned a set of Christmas plates, but Dusty threw them out when I was at Shore Lodge. But tossing my possessions in the trash and putting my bungalow up for sale while I was gone wasn't the worst thing he did. He left my dog at a shelter. Poor Buddy was abandoned while I was locked away with Nurse Wright.

I toss chicken bones in the trash, and Buddy trots inside, shaking his wet coat. Water droplets fly through the air, and we wince and groan. He comes over and licks my hand. I say, "You sweet dog."

"Max," I say as he runs into the kitchen, "close the front door and towel Buddy off, like I showed you."

"Okay," he says, leaving the room. The front door slams shut, and Max says, "I locked it, Grandma, to keep the bad guys out."

I glance at Dusty, who is bringing down champagne glasses from a high shelf that only he and I could reach without a stool. What my grandson doesn't realize is that the person I was trying to keep out is right here in my house.

Dusty and I lock eyes, and for a flicker of an instant, I see the little boy I loved. I nod to him, because the younger, innocent version of Dusty must be buried down deep inside, covered up by the grown greedy son I've been seeing since his dad died. I'm used to him swaggering around asking for money, but tonight is the first time he's tried to diminish me and tell falsehoods to friends and family since I swam in frigid water and made it home. I'd better be on my toes every second around him.

I lean over to Mary and whisper in her ear. "Let's talk later."

Dusty says, "Be right back. Don't lock the door. I'm stepping out for a smoke."

He strides out, and I stare at his back, smelling treachery and deceit wafting off him. I get the feeling if I'm not careful, he'll try to take everything I've built. He's building a case with false stories designed to make me appear mentally incompetent. The next step is to take away my remaining money and my company. But with Fred having my durable power of attorney, I'm probably protected from my son's grasping, greedy gimme-gimme grimy reaching paws.

I bite my lip. I must be on my toes tonight and watch what I say. On Monday, I'll speak with the city planning department about how to speed up the project. The sooner I build Stone Estates and prove myself in my new work capacity, the better. But with a lack of construction experience, am I a fool to proceed on this new venture?

I tap a toe. I ran a profitable garden store in the past. Surely I'm sharp enough to tackle building Stone Estates.

9

FRANKIE

Light jazz plays in the background, and I nod to Special Agent Mark Brick, who I invited over for dinner because we're both bumping around without family in the area for the holiday. The store-bought pumpkin pie is delicious, but my favorite part is the whipped cream on top. When my phone rings, I let my fork clatter to the plate and glance at caller ID. "It's Fishbone's ex-wife. Wonder why she's calling."

Mark frowns. "Too bad Fishbone got hurt. Sure changed his life."

I wave away his comment and answer the phone. "Special Agent McNalley. How can I help you?"

Irena says in a tense, hoarse voice, "My daughter Kelly was taken by my father, and he was just released from prison. I don't know where he's taken her and I'm terrified. Will you find her? Please?"

I wait a beat, mulling it over.

She clears her throat. "Violet's looking into this, but you're the experts. Can you help? I don't know what to do. She's gone."

"When did this happen?"

She coughs. "When I was out on my boat, probably sometime this afternoon, but I'm not sure exactly when he took her."

I shoot my partner Mark a look because in my book, Christmas Eve isn't a day to roam or leave a thirteen-year-old home alone. If I had a teenage girl, I'd keep close watch to prevent an impromptu party popping up while a parent is gone, given your typical adolescent kind of trouble.

I sigh. It seems an FBI Agent's work is never done, even on Christmas Eve. "I'll put you on speaker. Special Agent Brick is here, and it'd be good for him to listen to what you have to tell us."

10

———

IRENA

I pace back and forth in the living room, chastising myself for not staying home with my daughter all day. Instead, I tried to be a hero and paid more attention to my friends than Kelly. Sure, I helped Jacklyn cross Cedar Channel to sneak into Shore Lodge, but my daughter needed me more.

I shake my head at how I overlooked the danger signs. My dad is dangerous. He's an angry, vengeful man, and I should've realized he might take Kelly to get back at me.

I brush away my stray thoughts and say to Special Agent Frankie McNalley, "Put me on speaker. That's fine. And thank you for taking my call on Christmas Eve."

She says, "Start from the beginning and tell us what happened."

"I was out for the day helping friends, and when I came home, Kelly was gone. When I was young, my dad killed a man in a bar fight, and he was sent to prison. My mom and I moved away without telling him where we went. He has a horrible temper and he used to hit my mom."

"I'm sorry to hear that. Then what happened?"

"My dad got out of prison and recently showed up in town demanding to see me. I didn't want to re-connect, but he came to my house and walked in like he owned the place. I kicked him out, and he's been angry at me ever since."

She says, "We'll check to see if he was released on parole, for starters. Give us his full name. Coming to Millersville may have violated his parole agreement,"

"The last name is Pickle, Leonard Hornsby Pickle."

Agent Brick speaks up. "Have you checked to see if your daughter is at a friend's house instead of with your father?"

I stride into the kitchen and stare at my dad's note encased in a plastic Ziplock bag to preserve fingerprints. "Kelly didn't take her phone, which never happens, and her friend said she never showed up. I don't have a cell number for my dad. He left a note saying not to contact the police."

McNalley says, "Read the note to us."

I read the note aloud, and she says, "How old is your daughter?"

My throat closes tight with tears. "Kelly is only thirteen."

"And your father was convicted of murder?"

"Yes."

"I'll run it by my boss, but I believe we can treat this as a kidnapping. Your father may have crossed state lines with your daughter and violated his parole."

I gulp, imagining Kelly handcuffed in the car. "Please, do something."

Brick says, "We will. You made the right call, getting in touch with us. We need to get on this right away."

I wipe my moist palms on my jeans. "Will you issue an Amber Alert?"

McNalley says, "What kind of car is he driving?"

I study the ceiling, trying to recall. "A gray sedan. It didn't look new."

"No license plate number?"

I shake my head. "Not that I remember."

"Washington State plates?"

"I'm not sure, but I think so."

Brick says, "Sit tight, and we'll be in touch."

"Oh, wait, one more thing. My father always talked about running away to Canada and starting over."

McNalley says, "That's good to know. Text me a recent photo of Kelly with her full name, height and weight. What was she wearing the last time you saw her?"

I cringe and race into her bedroom, scanning the room. "She was wearing a blue bathrobe when I left this morning." Tears stream down my cheeks. I blurt out, "I don't know what she was wearing when he took her because I was gone all day."

"Check her phone for selfies taken today and send them to me. And check her socials for postings. Maybe your dad tagged her in a photo."

I clench my fists and sob. "He can't get away with this."

11

ROSE

Fred, Mary, Mercury and Mom help me clean the kitchen, and then I check on Max. He towels off Buddy, and the dog licks his hand. Despite my best intentions, this holiday evening has become a big fat fiasco due to my brother's dogged determination to wear Mom down. He's hurting Mom with taunts and relishing his role. What a jerk.

I glance at my brother, who is checking his phone and lounging on the new living room sofa Mom had to buy after he threw out her worn brown plaid one, and go over to him.

I loom over him until he glances up. "Hey, sis."

Shaking a finger at him, I say, "Don't treat Mom this way. She deserves better, especially on Christmas Eve. Don't put her down or make her friends question her mental acuity. She's fine and it's her favorite holiday. Back off."

He blinks and smiles. "I don't know what you're talking about. Now if you don't mind, I have important business to attend to." He stares at his phone.

I'd like to grab his phone and stomp on it, but I keep my voice down and say, "Don't hurt Mom. You already tried to ruin her life once. Be kind."

Max comes over. "What're you talking about?"

Dusty ruffles my son's hair. "Nothing, just boring grown-up stuff. Have you seen this trick I can do with a quarter? I can make it disappear, just like that."

Max sits down and watches Dusty pull a quarter from his pocket and put it in his hand. He switches the quarter from hand to hand and says, "Which hand is it in? This one or that one?" He holds out his clenched hands, where the knuckles are red and raw.

Max and Buddy stare at my brother's closed hands. Max points to one, and Dusty opens his hands. "You're right. There you go, it's yours."

Max grins and pockets the coin. "Thanks." He hops up, finds a plastic dog toy and tosses it across the room for Buddy.

Striding into the kitchen to see what else I can do, I fume under my breath at my brother for badgering Mom, but I also sense the stirrings of familiar sibling rivalry. I'd hoped to be the center of attention tonight as Mom's surprise dinner guest, but my brother upstaged me. Dusty claimed all of my parents' attention since the day he was born, while I was expected to smile, stay on the sidelines, get good grades and not make waves, because my brother made more than enough trouble for two of us.

Drying a dish, I say in a low voice to Mom, "Sorry about how Dusty is acting. I wish he wasn't so mean to you."

Mom shrugs. "It's no problem. I've been through it before. Nothing I can't handle, but thanks for your support."

She turns and hugs me tight, enveloping me in her warm arms. I sigh and lean into her strength, hoping to be as strong as her when I face obstacles.

Mom pats my back. "I appreciate who you are and how you support me. You are a special, wonderful daughter, and I'm lucky to have you in my life."

A tear slides down my cheek, and I step back and sniffle, wiping my eyes. "Merry Christmas, Mom."

She pats my cheek. "Merry Christmas, dear one. I love you."

Max runs in, followed by Buddy, and he wraps his arms around me. "Why're you crying, Mom?"

I smile through my tears and say, "I just heard something I've always wanted to hear, and I'm happy."

Dusty stomps into the kitchen. "Sorry to break up your happy little group, but where am I sleeping tonight?"

Mom says, "I think it'd be best if you went home. It's safe for you to drive."

His jaw clenches. "I'm not leaving. The snow's too deep. I'll stay in my old bedroom. It's all set up for me."

Max claps his hands. "That's where we're sleeping. We'll camp out together."

Mom and I shoot each other a quick look and roll our eyes. I brought my son to a Christmas celebration that has been turned into a nightmare by my moody, manipulating brother.

12

DEL

I pull on my coat and step outside for a breath of fresh air. Stuck indoors with contentious people has put me on edge, making my back muscles tense and tight. I stretch my arms in the cold night air and find myself missing the still silence of my room at Shore Lodge. My phone rings, and I flinch at the sudden sound, pulling it from my pocket.

My brother is calling, and I frown as I answer. "Hello?"

He says in a jolly voice, "Just wanted to wish you a Merry Christmas. How's life at Shore Peaks?"

I shake my head. "It's called Shore Lodge, and I left."

"You left? I thought you were going to live there until you croaked and leave me all your money." He laughs, but I don't join in. He had already taken all that was dear to me in a selfish moment, thinking only of himself.

The silence stretches across the miles, as it has since

he visited our home when my wife was going through chemotherapy. I'd told him not to stop by if he was sick, but while I was out grocery shopping for something she could eat, he let himself in with his emergency key and coughed and sneezed all over my wife until I arrived home and sent him packing. My own brother ignored the firm house rules I set up to protect my wife, who had a severely compromised immune system. She caught his bug, went into the hospital and never came home.

"Del, you still there?"

I shiver and stare at snow, which looks to be about two feet deep and is still coming down with big, fat flakes. A streetlight sheds light, slicing through winter darkness. Dr. Henderson at Shore Lodge suggested I consider forgiving my brother for killing my wife, but I don't want to. It feels better to harbor a grudge than to accept that she exited the planet years too soon. "Yeah, I'm still here."

"Feels like something's off between us, you know? Are you upset with me about something? You didn't invite me to the memorial service and didn't speak to me when I got there. What's going on? Let's clear this up. I miss you, man."

I blow out a breath. Wind blows snow in my face, and I blink back tears. "Something's bugging me, you got that right, but this isn't the time to talk about it."

"Come on, it's been bugging me. What's up with you?"

"Not everything's about you and how you feel, you know."

"Just get it off your chest. I can take it."

I'm about to let my brother have it when the door swings open, and Jacklyn's son steps outside. "I'll tell you some other time."

"Merry Christmas," my brother says in a chipper voice. "Come by our house tomorrow. We'll have Christmas chili and cornbread."

My grip tightens on the phone. I'd like to strangle him for what he did, taking my life away, ripping it from my heart with his inconsiderate actions. If he was less self-centered, he'd realize he should feel shame. He'd know what he did.

"Night," I say and hang up on him as he says, "See you then?"

I grit my teeth and watch wind rush down the street, swirling snow. My brother is snug in his cozy home with his healthy wife, but I'm bitter and serving time in this solitary cell of grief, fueled by resentment and anger. No way I'll forgive him, even if he begs me on bended knee.

Dusty takes a drag from his cigarette and slowly exhales smoke. "Sounded like you were getting into it with someone in that call. I don't mean to butt in, but who were you speaking with?"

I shake my head. "My brother."

He nods. "Feels good to blame someone else for your problems, doesn't it? I should know. Mom's the target for my anger."

I cringe, because I thought Jacklyn's son was a whack-job with no self-awareness. But comparing me to him makes me wince. Am I similar to Dusty, with his unresolved issues? I dearly hope not. But it occurs to me that I could be a lot like the tall brooding man standing beside me, shrugging off the cold in a flannel shirt and jeans. If I'm brutally honest, it feels good to aim my anger at someone, but deep down I know there's really no one to blame. It just happened, and if it hadn't been my brother, she might've succumbed to something else. I could've brought home a virus from touching the handle of the grocery cart at the store. By holding a grudge against my brother, I'm just like Dusty. Maybe it's time I revisited my outlook on my wife's death.

13

VIOLET

I unlock the door to my company, Outrigger Services, and Karina and Bernard follow me inside. I point to the bull pen. "Make yourselves at home. I'll get my computer and join you. I'd rather not call my team in on Christmas Eve, but if I have to, I will."

I sigh and hope I can deliver on my promise to Irena to bring Kelly back home. I'd rather not ask my team for help. Vincent is busy with his new baby, but there's a faint possibility Mimi and Flora might be willing to come in and assist.

Karina sets down food and pulls off her coat, tossing it on a chair. "Okay, thanks."

Bernard adjusts his black-framed glasses. "Just tell us what to do." He gives Karina a half-smile. "We've solved a mystery or two, haven't we, Karina?"

My sister beams. "We have. Let's do this."

Although I doubt two amateurs can be of much help, I nod. "Here's the plan. Karina, I want you to contact Irena's neighbors and go door to door asking if they have video surveillance."

She tilts her head. "We came with you. Can I borrow your car?"

I toss the keys to her, realizing I'm accustomed to relying on my professional team. Mimi typically handles the door-to-door boots-on-the-ground intelligence gathering. "Sure. And we need that intel fast. Every minute counts."

Bernard stands. "I'll go with her. They might take us more seriously if there's two of us, not just one person. We'll look less suspicious, approaching a house on a holiday."

I raise my eyebrows. "Good point."

Karina glances at the food. "Would it be okay if we ate dinner real fast before we go? It'd be a shame to let it go to waste, with it still being warm and all."

I shrug. "Sure, it won't take too long."

We open containers we brought along, shovel in mouthfuls, and soon Karina and Bernard are heading out the door. I call, "Text me with what you're hearing. Keep me updated as you go house to house. Stay in touch."

Karina smiles. "We will. Don't worry, sis, we're on the case. We'll find Kelly."

"Good, because that's what I told Irena. See if you can get her dad's license plate. Be safe out there in the snow.

It's coming down hard. I may need to call two members of my team to get a jump on this right out of the gate."

The door closes, and I lock it behind them. I open my laptop to check the U.S. border crossing into Canada for a gray sedan, and my phone dings. Irena texted to say she's contacting the FBI agent she met when her ex-husband, Jack Fishbone, was in trouble. That was a big mess, but we finally got it straightened out.

I text her back. "Sounds good. Keep me in the loop."

I glance outside, where snow is drifting down. My all-terrain vehicle is fine in snow, so Karina will be able to navigate the short distance to Irena's neighborhood. I furrow my brow and realize it might've been best if I had gone with them. They're not experienced investigators and could miss important details. Rubbing my aching temples, where a headache is making its presence known, I wince at how I sent out two greenhorns. I need my team to do this right.

I send a text to Mimi and Flora. 'Is there any way you could spare a few hours this evening to come in on a special project? Irena's daughter Kelly is missing. I know it's Christmas Eve, but I thought I'd ask since you know her.'

My phone immediately lights up, dinging with two responses.

Mimi writes, 'Count me in."

Flora texts, 'I'd come, but my car would get stuck in the snow.'

Mimi chimes in. 'I'll pick you up in five. We'll be there soon, boss.'

I settle back in my seat, letting out a slow breath and nodding to myself. Everything is going to work out fine. My team, with the exception of Vincent staying home with his baby, will help. Together we'll nail this callous grandfather who had no right to take his innocent granddaughter away from her home.

14

KARINA

I climb in Violet's car, and Bernard slides into the passenger seat. He looks over. "We've got this, right? No problem for our dynamic duo." I chuckle and drive down snowy streets to Irena's. "By the time we're done talking to neighbors, Violet will want to hire us."

No one else is out in this weather, and the streets are deserted. A hush falls over the car. Wiper blades flick back and forth, clearing fast-falling snow from the windshield. I turn the defroster up to high and let out a sigh. "Kelly must be scared out of her mind. I hope we'll find her right away."

He coughs, wiping his eyes. "I do too. I hope this experience won't mark her forever."

As we lumber along through snow to Irena's house, it feels much farther than a mile from downtown. A blast of wind bears down, and the car shudders. Gripping the wheel tight, I lean forward to see better.

Bernard clears his throat. "Would you like me to drive?"

"No, I'm fine. Violet gave me the keys, and she's my sister, so I'm responsible if anything happens to her car."

"Just be careful. Gigi would take me to an early grave if she knew I let you drive in these conditions. I hope we'll find some useful information."

I blow out a breath. "Me too. Irena must be going nuts. Those two are close."

Bernard fiddles with his glasses. "I wonder if anyone's told Jack? I'd want to know if my daughter was taken."

I cringe and wonder if Jack knows. Irena's ex-husband is recovering from traumatic brain injury, and it's possible Irena didn't tell him, so he wouldn't worry and get upset.

Snow crunches under our tires, and I pull over and park outside Irena's house. We open the car doors, pushing against accumulated snow. Houses along the street covered with snow look like a fairytale scene, but we know what happened here is a darker story.

My pulse picks up, and I stride through snow, making my way to Irena's house. "Let's talk with Irena before we check with the neighbors."

He nods and hunches over as he walks. "The weather's not ideal, but we'll get this done, just like when you searched for Gigi's missing journal."

I tilt my head but don't bother to mention that a stolen

diary is much different than a girl being taken. We all know the stakes are high in Kelly's situation, but there's no need to state the obvious. I reach out and pat his shoulder. "I'm glad that finding the journal brought us together. We make a good team."

He smiles. "I feel the same way."

We approach the front steps, and Irena runs out of the house, hair flying, arms flailing. "She's gone! Help me find her. Kelly's been taken."

I stomp snow off my boots. "We will. Violet sent us."

We cross the threshold, entering a house that's missing part of its heart, and I vow to do everything I can to bring Kelly home. If there's one bit of information we can gather from neighbors to help Violet solve the case, we'll find it. I'm not trained as a detective, but I'll do everything in my power to uncover threads connecting us to the truth.

I give Irena a hug, and she weeps in my arms. I whisper, "We'll find Kelly. I'm sure of it."

15

VIOLET

At the sound of a key in the lock at Outrigger Services, I jump up and hurry to the door. Mimi comes in, rosy-cheeked, followed by Flora. They drop their coats on the back of their chairs in the bullpen, and Mimi says, "Hey, boss. Tell us what's going on."

Flora says in her high-pitched voice, "Yeah, what happened and who's doing what?"

I pace the floor. "Here's what we know. Irena's thirteen-year-old daughter Kelly was taken by her grandfather, who she just met. He killed a man and was recently released from prison on the east side of the mountains and just showed up in town. Our only lead is that he's driving a gray sedan."

I pick up a blue erasable marker and write key facts on

a white board mounted on the wall. Kelly. Grandfather is a convicted felon. Gray sedan.

Mimi pulls her hair back in a pony tail. "License plate number?"

I make a face. "No idea, but I sent Karina from the café and Bernard Frackus out to canvas the neighborhood and see if anyone has video surveillance, or if they saw something. We're after a license plate number and the approximate time they left Irena's house to get a better picture of where they might be."

Mimi frowns. "You sent two civilians out? Are you sure that was a good idea?"

I nod. "I hear you. It might not have been my best decision, but they're driving my car, so they should be fine."

Mimi glances outside. "When will snowplows clear the roads?"

I snort. "I have no idea. The town has one snow plow, because it rarely snows. So we could be socked in for a day or more."

Flora half-smiles. "Small town living at its best. It's a good night to stay inside and read a book."

"Except we don't have that luxury tonight. Mimi, why don't you check the border crossings? Flora, keep an eye on chat rooms and socials for postings. It's a long shot, but we may find something to help nail down their location."

I wipe my palms on my pants. Our gulped down dinner

sits heavy in my stomach, and there was no time to cele-brate the holiday or enjoy the flavor of the food. "There'll be no relaxing until we find Kelly. Any questions?"

"No, boss."

I steal a glance at the street and worry that I made a mistake by sending my café-owning sister and her retired science teacher friend out together. But then I open my laptop and get to work. I'll liaise with FBI Special Agent McNalley, if they've taken on Kelly's case, when we find something to relay.

16

IRENA

When a car stops out front, I dash outside, waving my hands and expecting to see Violet emerge from her vehicle. I bite back tears when Karina and Bernard climb out of the car and march through snow to my house. I doubt any sleuthing done by a café owner and a retired high school science teacher will help me find my daughter. I blow out a breath and suppose Violet was too busy in the office to come. But that's a good sign, because I need her using her sharply-honed skills to track my horrible father down.

My voice trembles when I say, "Help me find my daughter. Kelly's missing."

They stomp their feet and come inside. Bernard shoves his hands in his coat pockets. Karina gives me a hug and then she steps back. "Violet sent us to ask your neighbors if they saw anything."

Bernard nods. "We're going to canvas the neighborhood for clues."

Inside I'm screaming and terrified to my core for Kelly, not knowing where she went with a grandfather she just met. I manage to say, "Do you know anything yet?"

Karina glances at Bernard and shakes her head. "Not yet. We'd better get going to interview people before they forget what they saw."

"If they saw anything," he says. "Every minute counts in situations like this. I've seen it on TV shows."

I suppress a groan. These two know nothing about how to save a teenage girl who was taken by a cruel blood relative. "I'll go too and help you."

Karina holds up a hand. "Violet said for you to stay home in case Kelly comes home or the FBI calls or stops by."

Bernard adjusts his black-framed glasses. "We'd better get going."

My chest grows tight as they march away through the snow. I want to go with them and take action. I hate sitting on my hands doing nothing to bring my daughter home. I wish I could drive and follow my father to hunt him down, but I don't know where they went. "Call me if you find anything."

"We will," Karina says in a clear, calm voice.

They march off arm in arm, and I close the door, leaning against it, my heart racing. I rest a hand on my stomach, where my dad punched it when I was a child. I must bring Kelly home before she experiences my father's wrath first-hand. His nickname was Rattlesnake for how fast he lashed out with his fists.

17

KARINA

We stomp through snow and climb up three steps to Irena's next door neighbor's house. Bernard rings the doorbell, and the door swings open. A woman in her sixties with a blond bob cocks her head. "Oh dear, I heard Kelly's missing. Irena just called to let me know."

I nod. "It's awful. We were sent by Outrigger Services to see if anyone saw when Kelly's grandfather took her."

She squints and frowns, looking down, as if deep in thought.

Bernard says, "Did you happen to see a gray sedan at Irena's house? We need his license plate number."

I shift my weight, standing on the porch. Cold seeps into my favorite pair of worn boots. "Do you happen to have video surveillance on your doorbell?"

She shakes her head. "It's horrible, what happened.

And no, I don't have it because nothing bad happens here. This was a safe, happy spot to live in until now."

Bernard chimes in. "Did you see anything unusual late this morning or this afternoon? We're trying to pinpoint the exact time when he took Kelly."

She brightens. "Why yes, I heard a car stop next door, and I glanced out the window, not wanting to spy on Irena, mind you, but to keep an eye on the neighborhood. I'm retired and don't have much going on except for gardening. I was a teacher."

Bernard beams. "So was I. I taught high school science, how about you?"

"Fifth grade."

"I thought you looked familiar."

They smile at each other, and I stand in the cold, wanting to extract information from this woman and move on to other houses. I clear my throat, hoping to break up their mutual admiration society, and turn the subject toward Kelly. "You heard a car and then what?"

The neighbor says, "I did, and I noticed a gray sedan parked in Irena's driveway. A man got out and went to the door. I think Kelly let him in, from what I saw."

I cringe. Is it possible Kelly went willingly with him?

Bernard tilts his head. "Was it a two-door or four-door sedan? What color of gray was it?"

She shrugs. "Who knows about the color. Gray is gray, right? But it was a four-door sedan, I can tell you that. He opened the trunk and pulled something out before going to the front door. It looked like a guitar case."

I whoosh out a breath. Finally, we're getting somewhere. Irena and Violet will be interested in hearing this. "If you had to, would you describe the color of his car as a dark gray or light gray?"

She taps her lips. "I'm not sure. Maybe light gray?

I nod. "Thank you. We might be back for more information later on."

Bernard shakes her hand. "It was a pleasure to meet you. I'm Bernard."

"I'm Kathy." She pats her blond hair worn in a bob cut and waves goodbye.

We turn and step down the stairs, hurrying to the next house.

18

DUSTY

I rub my right cheek and frown, standing outside with the older guy from Shore Lodge. Taking a drag of my cigarette, I say, "I should call Nurse Wright and tell her where you are. Bet she'd like to know. They'll come by in a flash and get you, bringing you back."

His body stiffens, and he crosses his arms. "It won't make a difference if you make that call, because I wasn't on her floor. I admitted myself and left, so it's no big deal. And I know what you're up to. I don't like it one bit. Stop trying to throw your weight around. This is supposed to be a nice evening with family and friends, and you're souring the mood."

I toss the cigarette butt in the snow and turn to him, blowing smoke in his face. "I don't know what you're talking about, old man. I'm just here to have a meal and spend quality time with my family. You're a stranger, and there's no reason for you to be here. You don't belong. You shouldn't speak up and tell me what to do if you're not one of us."

The guy with big ears coughs and points a finger at me. "Stop deluding yourself. It's obvious you're not wanted at that table. Everyone inside can see that. You're a little boy in a big man's body, stomping on anyone in your path. You're lashing out at how your life turned out, desperate to regain control."

I clear my throat. "You might be right, but that wasn't nice to say, little man, especially on a holiday."

"The truth had to be told."

I stare at trees swaying in the wind and take a deep breath, turning to stride into a house where no one wants me, slamming the door in his face.

19

—————

JACKLYN

y pulse picks up when Dusty opens the door and stomps in the house with his boots on. He brushes snow off his shoulders and says, "Is there a place we can go talk?"

I purse my lips and tell myself not to be bullied by my own flesh and blood. "I don't feel safe with you, not with your obvious anger and after what you did to me. We'll talk right here." I sit on the sofa, patting the seat beside me.

His eyes narrow, and he crosses his arms, standing. His face flushes and his jaw tenses, but I stay where I am and don't say a word. This is my home, and he entered my house uninvited, so he can play by my rules.

Buddy comes over, pushing his head against my knee, and I lean over and pet him. He looks up at me with big brown eyes. This sweet dog has been such a comfort to me since my husband died. We support each other, which is more than I say for my son.

Mercury gets up from an armchair. "If you need me, I'll be in the dining room."

Dusty clears his throat. "We don't need you pops. We're fine as we are. Isn't that right, Mom?"

Rose slides into a seat next to me. "If you're doing this, I'm going to be here too. You're my family, and all that's left of it."

I nod to her. "I appreciate your support. Come on, Dusty, let's do this."

He paces the room, and a crazy wild notion races through my mind. I grimace and picture myself grabbing the fireplace poker as a weapon to whack his broad shoulders. I'm horrified at this self-righteous misguided man who locked me away in a warehouse of lost souls.

Dusty shakes a fist. "I want my company back. I built it, and I deserve to run it."

Fred comes in and stands behind me, resting a hand on my shoulder. "Dusty, your mother rightfully took it when you abused your power of attorney and spent her money on yourself."

Dusty glares, and a vein in his temple throbs. "Everything I did was for her."

Fred says, "That's an outright lie. You sent her to a locked mental institution and left her there to die. How could that benefit her?"

I shake my head. "Sorry, Dusty, but what you're saying

isn't cutting it, not tonight when the truth is on the table. It's time to clear the air. You tricked me into going to Shore Lodge and admitted me against my will. You sold my store and bought land that I now own for a subdivision. You used my money to buy a new truck that you totaled. You can't argue with the facts."

He flings his hands up in the air, bringing back memories of when he was eight years old and arguing about anything and everything. He didn't want to rake the lawn on Sunday afternoons, when we all went out and did yardwork. He didn't want to carry customer purchases from the store to their cars when he was fifteen. He didn't want to come in for dinner when it was served. I blink back tears and brush away memories to focus on the greedy beast standing before me.

His eyes grow wide. "It's not my fault the truck got wrecked."

I arch an eyebrow. "Be accountable and take responsibility, like I taught you."

He turns to the window, hands clenched. I wish the snow would turn to rain, so Dusty would get in his truck and leave. I want him out of my house.

Fred says, "Your mother is the legal owner of Stone Construction. I've known you a long time, son, and it's time to take your life in a new direction, maybe in a new town. Move on and begin again. Your father would want that for you."

Dusty frowns. "Don't tell me what to do. I'm not a kid

anymore. And you didn't know my Dad like you thought you did. I knew him best."

We're silent for a beat, because there's no need to reply to his blatant selfishness.

Putting his hands together, Dusty says in a pleading tone, "Mom, you know I have to be my own boss. That's what I do best. Please give me back my company."

I shake my head. "You lost your bond with the state. I doubt anyone would hire an unbonded and unlicensed contractor known for ripping his mother off."

Dusty scowls, rubbing his right cheek. "Tell you what, give me the land back free and clear for Stone Estates, and I'll put in the sewer lines and utilities. I'll sell it to a developer and split the profits with you eighty-twenty."

I tip my head back and laugh. "That land is mine, and no one will take it from me. Fred's right. Go do something else with your life."

Dusty jabs a finger at Fred. "This is your fault for meddling in family matters. You should never have helped her. I'll get you back for that."

Fred says in a steely voice, "Don't mess with me, son, or you'll regret it. This is the last time you'll get away with threatening me or your mother. She's been very kind until now. Remember, we can get a restraining order to keep you off the premises."

I chime in. "I could've done that before, but I didn't want to freeze you out entirely as my son, and I wanted to give you a chance to prove you could be a better person. I believed you could turn your attitude around, but your visit tonight isn't showing your best side. It's clear you have no remorse."

He crosses his arms and glares, sweat beading on his brow.

Rose says, "Mom's right, Dusty. She's given you every chance to make amends for how you treated her after Dad died. Don't blow this, or she'll get a no contact order. Just apologize for what you did, and we can all move on like nothing ever happened."

I rub Buddy's soft ears and cock my head, considering her suggestion. I doubt there will be any moving on after what Dusty did. My heart is hardening and turning to stone, given his unrepentant attitude during this discussion.

Gazing at my son, I say in a clear, calm voice, "I won't ever forget how you locked me away and sold my store out from underneath me. Those ugly facts about under-handed dealings are burned into my brain. But I would like to hear you say you're sorry. Maybe after that, we could begin to move on."

Dusty stares at the fireplace, scuffing his big brown boot on my new tan carpet, leaving dirt marks. He frowns, shoving his hands in his pockets. "Mom, I'm sorry for how it worked out. Now can I get my company back?"

20

DUSTY

My mom and sister sit on the couch, side by side, bringing me back to my childhood, when the two of them united against me, and Rose acted like my second mother. I let out a slow breath and tell myself to remain calm. To achieve my goal of regaining my company, I've got to bend to their pressure and bow down to the matriarchy, appeasing my mother.

I offer an apology, using my most sincere expression, and wait. Mom tilts her head and doesn't say anything, but I didn't expect her to jump up and sign the company over to me on the spot. I'll wait her out, like I did as a kid, and she'll give in.

Gazing at Mom, Rose, Fred, Mary and Max, who is sitting on the living floor by Buddy, I glancing in the dining room and nod to Mercury and Del. Clapping my hands, I say, "This concludes the most recent episode of the Stone Family Feud. You can go back to what you were doing. Mom, it's time for you to sign papers giving me the company. Fred can help you do that. All right with you, Fred?"

The fire pops, and tension in the room fairly crackles. No one moves.

Fred frowns. "No, it's not all right with me. It's not in her best interests. You can forget that idea right now."

I eye him. "I did a little research that might change your mind. Do you want everyone here to know who you were having drinks with last Wednesday when you should've been home?"

He shifts his weight from side to side and studies his shoes.

Mary touches his arm. "Fred, what's he talking about?"

Fred shakes his head and runs a hand through his thinning hair.

Mary stares at him. "Why won't you tell me? Who were you with? Just tell me if it was a client or not."

He grimaces. "It wasn't a client, but that's all I'm going to say."

Mom stands and puts her hands on her hips. "I won't give you back the company or the land. I own Stone Construction, and I'll take the project to the finish line, no matter what obstacles appear in my path. So, back off, buster, and find something else to do. I won't be a victim you bully and push around. Intimidation tactics won't work on me."

I rub my right cheek and wish I'd picked a violent course of action, such as taking revenge with fondue forks or wrapping ropes around my mother and torturing her until she agreed to sign documents turning over Stone Construction to the rightful owner.

We stare at each other, eyes locked and jaws tight, but look away when someone knocks and opens the door, coming in from the cold. Bernice is wearing a white knit cap, and she's bundled up in a big black puffer jacket.

Mom rushes over and hugs Bernice, a long-time friend of my folks who runs an escrow company. I make a face because Bernice worked behind the scenes to skewer my plans of selling this house until Mom and Fred arrived and stopped the sale. Everywhere I turn, Mom is a boulder on the trail, blocking my path to success.

Bernice hangs her coat on a hook by the door. She pats her short gray hair and straightens her black blazer worn over white pants.

Bernice grins. "And this is my friend Marsha."

The others say, "Hi Marsha."

Mary goes over to hug Bernice, and others crowd around, but I sink into an armchair, scratch my stubbled chin and feel like the odd man out. I don't belong in this house. I don't belong in this town. I don't belong anywhere else.

Bernice comes over. "Hi, Dusty."

I cock my head and try to wrest back control. "Hey, Bernice. How's it going?"

She opens her arms and smiles. "It's wild weather outside. I'm surprised we got here in one piece."

Blowing out a sigh, I consider my next steps in the plan to take my company away from my mom. But with her friends gathering around her, giving her support, my chances of success tonight are slim and fading fast.

Bernice says, "I hope you don't hold a grudge against me for delaying the sale of your mom's house by twenty minutes. I was only doing the right thing. Let's not let it get between us, okay?"

I clench my jaw because grudges are what I do best, besides building beautiful houses. With a scowl, I say, "You ruined the deal I set up. I needed that money."

She steps back and eyes me, folding her arms. "That couple walked on the deal as soon as they learned you stole money from your mother and stuck her on Cedar Island, so you could sell her place. It wouldn't have held up in court under the circumstances."

"Whatever."

She says, "I haven't seen you in town much."

"I had to move. I live in Foothills now."

She smiles. "It must be pretty up there by the mountains."

I shrug, flung back in time to being a sullen teenager. Being in this house reminds me of my childhood, where I was alone but surrounded by a band of three merry family members. I look her in the eye. She could be my meal ticket. "I'd rather live in Millersville. Do you need to hire someone at the escrow company? I could work for you."

She flinches. "We do have an opening, but I'm afraid that's not a good idea, not after how you treated your mother. Because I have to be able to trust my employees, especially with the money that comes through our accounts. Trust is everything to me, and that's part of why I love your mom. She's one of the most trustworthy people I know."

I resist the urge to roll my eyes at her fan club and lean forward, resting my hands on my knees. "I'll change. I can learn to do office work. I'll dress differently."

She tilts her head. "Sorry, but it's a solid no from me. You're better off doing what you do best, which is building."

I say in a whiny voice, "But no one will hire me."

She glances over at the others, crowding around the entry. "I bet something will work out. Just keep trying."

She walks away and exclaims in a loud voice how glad she is to see everyone. Introductions are made, and the chatter of many voices swirls around me, alone in a solitary whirlpool of woe and worries. Mom's dog sits and stares at me, as if he's judging me for leaving him at a shelter, and I bury my head in my hands.

Mom says to Bernice, "How did you get here? I thought the roads weren't clear."

Bernice laughs. "It didn't stop us, did it, Marsha?"

They chuckle, reminding me of how much I'd like to have someone in my life to share laughter and love. But here I sit, by myself, with no romantic prospects on the horizon.

Mom says, "Dusty, I bet you could make it to your cabin tonight. The snow isn't so bad. Bernice was able to drive."

I cough to cover up the familiar sting of rejection and wounds that come from my mother not wanting me around. "I'm staying here tonight, but thanks for thinking of my well-being, on a highway with bald tires traveling in deep snow on icy roads. Thanks a lot, Mom."

She flicks a glance at my sister and her friends, and I swallow tears and stand, walking through a suddenly silent room toward the bathroom. Man, I miss my dad. If only he hadn't died, my life wouldn't be upside down. I've got to win Mom over to my side, so she'll see things the way I do. Dad was always the one to convince her, but he's long gone.

I close the bathroom door and lock it. Sitting on the closed toilet lid, I let tears stream down my cheeks. How am I going to get myself out of this mess?

21

MERCURY

I hunker down in a chair at the dining table and tug on my mustache. Dusty and Jacklyn are talking in the living room, and I'll jump up and butt in if I think it's called for. But given their complex family dynamics, I'm staying out of it for now. She's surrounded by steady long-term friends, and I admire her for creating long-lasting bonds. I could learn from her that way.

Del slides into a chair next to me and says in a low voice, "Pretty messed up, aren't they? They're never going to see eye to eye. But they keep butting their heads."

I lean over to him. "Jacklyn's holding out a tiny ray of hope for reconciliation, but I don't see it coming. Must be every mother's hope, to have a family that gets along."

Del coughs into his hand.

I cock my head. "Something I said?"

He nods. "Almost. I've got family problems of my own,

so who am I to talk? Jacklyn and her kids could go to family counselling to try and get this worked out."

I shake my head and sigh. "There's no healing this, from what I see. How can you morph years of harboring bitterness into accepting differences and respect? I don't think the math works out on that one, sad to say."

The door opens and two middle-aged women come in, shivering from the cold. A gust of wind blows in snow and cold air before Jacklyn shuts the door. Her bungalow is full to the brim and can barely hold more people.

Jacklyn rushes over, greets her friend with a hug and meets the other woman with a warm smile. I don't think Jacklyn's ever met a stranger, she's so outgoing.

Del and I stand and make our way to the crowded entry, ready to join the strange Christmas Eve party. Glancing around the larger group, I hope we won't get stranded here in the storm. The tense Stone family dynamics aren't a recipe for having a relaxing time cooped up together under one roof, and I don't trust her son not to make trouble. Dusty gives off a bad vibe like he might erupt into violence at any minute. His grudge against the world is aimed at his mother, making him potentially dangerous. I'll keep watch and protect Jacklyn in case desperate Dusty tries something. I might be wrong, but it's possible he may have murder on his mind.

22

IRENA

While Karina and Bernard go door to door talking to my neighbors, I open my laptop in the living room and check social media for new posts by my daughter. Finding nothing, I stifle a sob. I check the U.S. Canadian border crossing cameras and look for a gray sedan in line but don't see a match. Shaking my head, I snap the laptop shut. I'm coming up dry, but Violet and the FBI agents are trying to track Kelly down.

I stand and open my hands wide. "Where are you, Kelly? Send me a sign, and let me know where you are. We're looking for you."

Kelly's phone dings, and I stride into the kitchen, picking it up. The phone is locked, but I key in the code.

Her best friend Plum texted. 'I thought you were coming over today. What happened?'

I call Plum, who picks up right away and says, "Why didn't you come over? I was waiting for you. We were going to make cookies."

My throat tightens with tears. "Listen, Plum, Kelly is missing and her grandfather took her. I don't know where she is. What time was she supposed to be at your house?"

"Two o'clock. We were going to make cookies with gluten free flour and no sugar. I thought Kelly liked her grandfather. Why are you worried? Won't he bring her back tonight?"

I sigh. "No, he isn't planning to. When was the last time you heard from Kelly? Did she tell you she was leaving town?"

"No, she didn't. It was really strange. But she did call and say one word."

I grip the phone tight. "What was it?"

"Safe."

My jaw drops. "Safe? That's what she said?"

"Yeah, I didn't get why she'd call and just say that and hang up."

I pace the kitchen, and my pulse pounds in my ears. "What time did she call and say that?"

"Maybe three or four, I'm not sure. I'm not good at keeping track of time. But I can look, hold on."

I wait a few seconds that feel like a lifetime, tapping my toe. The house is cold, and I miss the warmth of my daughter's beaming smile.

Plum comes back on the line. "She called to say that at

three, then she hung up. So it's a family thing that kept her away, it's not something to do with me?"

"That's right. Her not showing up has nothing to do with you, and everything to do with us, her family. Thank you for your help. If you hear from Kelly, please call me."

I give her my cell number and hang up. Grabbing my phone, I call Violet to tell her when Kelly was probably last in the house, before leaving town with my dad.

When Violet picks up on the first ring, I say, "I just learned Kelly was in the house at three o'clock. She used our secret password to tell her friend she was fine."

Violet says, "Got it. That helps. I'll pass that on to the FBI. Have you seen Karina and Bernard? They were supposed to be going door to door asking neighbors if they saw anything. We haven't heard from them yet, and my people usually report in by now."

"They stopped by when they were starting out. I'm sure they'll check in soon, or I hope they will. How about I go down the street and see if they've found anything?"

I start to pull on my boots, but Violet says, "No, we need you to stay home, in case your dad's plans change, and he brings Kelly back. It's a small chance, but we have to be ready for it. Keep your phone with you at all times."

I kick off my boots and slump down on the sofa. "Of course I will. Roger that."

"Hang in there. We'll get through this."

I bite my lip. "We will, and thanks for your help."

"You bet. That's what friends are for."

She hangs up, and I stare at the phone, wishing I'd asked her what progress she'd made, if any, so far. I make a pot of coffee and open my laptop, checking a social media site. Maybe if I post anonymously on the community page about Kelly going missing, that will bring in clues as to her whereabouts. I frown, because my posting that might attract comments from weirdos accusing me of not knowing where my own daughter is on a holiday afternoon.

Letting out a groan, I rest my head on the table, and tears trickle down my cheeks. I take a deep breath and straighten up, telling myself this is not a time for self-pity or recriminations. I've got to help find Kelly.

I pick up her phone to search who she contacted last and my jaw drops when I see she sent a text to an unknown number. Sent at one o'clock this afternoon, the text says, 'Home alone. What're you doing, Grandpa?'

My own daughter let the wolf into the house and welcomed him. She reached out and then he came by, intent on taking her when I wasn't home. I've got to tell Violet.

I pick up my phone with shaking hands and blame myself for letting this happen. But the good part is now that we have my dad's phone number, maybe they can track his movements and bring Kelly home.

23

KARINA

Bernard and I tromp through snow, side by side, matching each other's strides. I glance back at our footsteps and shake my head at how crazy it is that we're working together again and trying solving another problem. But this time, instead of searching for my grandmother's diary, we're after a missing person. Kelly is a great kid, and Irena is my friend, so I want to do all I can to bring them together again.

Bernard chuckles. "Pretty wild, isn't it? Your grandmother would be amazed that we're working together. She didn't want anyone to know we loved each other, but I was ready to tell the world about it."

A tear dribbles down my cheek, and I sniffle, pulling out a tissue and blowing my nose. "I wish she'd trusted me enough to tell me about you two. I would've been happy for her."

He cocks his head, and we turn, making our way up to the next house. "She said it was better kept it a secret. She didn't want the judgement that comes from small town gossip."

"It must've put a strain on you, not telling anyone."

He stops and takes off his glasses, wiping his eyes. "Gigi liked to say it was us against the world. The wind is making my eyes watery." He dabs a handkerchief to his nose.

"I know what you mean." We go up the steps, and I knock, but no one answers. I ring the doorbell twice and tap a toe, waiting.

"Coming," someone says from inside. "Don't be so impatient. I'm on my way."

I say to Bernard, "We should call Violet and tell her what we learned."

He nods. "Let's check in with her after this stop."

24

JACKLYN

My shoulders shudder when Dusty says he's staying and sleeping in my house tonight. A splitting headache makes me wince. I stand at the dining room window and take a moment to survey the snow-covered neighborhood. There's no hope of my son leaving in these conditions. We're trapped together tonight.

Bernice comes over and wraps her arms around me. "How's it going? I was surprised to see Dusty here."

I say in a low voice, "I didn't invite him, if that's what you mean, and I haven't changed my mind and forgiven him."

She pats my back. "You do what's best for you. I'll support you whatever your decision. People change, you know? Look at me, single for years, and now I have a partner." She grins and runs a hand through her short gray hair.

"How are the roads?"

"Icy and dangerous with almost two feet of snow and accumulating fast."

I cross my arms. "And it's still coming down. You might want to leave before you're stuck here all night. But of course, you and Marsha are always welcome here. You can stay and bunk in with the rest of us."

Dusty walks up to us, and his eyes are red. "Mom? Do you have a minute?"

I blow out a breath and tell myself to be kind and polite. That's what Karina would do. "Sure, what's up?"

Dusty says, "In private?"

Bernice squeezes my arm. "I'll get us beverages and settle in. Looks like we missed dinner. Did you have the fondue yet?"

Dusty nods. "The fondue party ended without a fork incident. We can count ourselves lucky to avoid a repeat of the sister attack."

I roll my eyes, because I still suspect he provoked Rose and brought it on himself.

Bernice walks out into the living room, and Dusty turns to me, wiping his eyes. "Look, Mom, I've been going about this all wrong. I'd like to apologize."

I cross my arms, ready to listen, but doubt he became a changed man in a matter of minutes. He's motivated by money most of all. I pat his arm. "I'm glad to hear that."

25

—————

KARINA

An older gentleman in a plaid knit vest, green slacks and green slippers opens the door. His gray eyebrows are thick and wild, and he peers at us. "What's all the fuss about?"

I gesture to Bernard to go ahead, and he says, "We're searching for a thirteen-year-old girl who was taken from two houses down earlier this afternoon."

The man cringes and runs a hand through his mop of gray hair. "Oh, dear. I can see why you're in such a hurry. How can I help?"

"Did you see anything unusual this afternoon?"

The man shakes his head. "No, I don't think so."

I speak up. "Did you hear anything, like someone screaming, by chance?"

"Nope, just the wind howling is all. We've got quite the

storm blowing through, don't we? Must be over two feet of snow." He starts to close his door. "Good luck."

I stick out a hand to stop him. "Wait, did you happen to see a gray sedan in the neighborhood?"

He rubs his stubbled chin. "Sure, I did, now that you mention it. The man asked if he could borrow snow chains for his car, which is odd, if you ask me. He should've had his own."

Bernard shoots me a look before asking, "Did he say where he was headed?"

The man shrugs. "Something about going over a pass? He mumbled a lot and wouldn't look me in the eye, so I'm not sure. He had tattoos on his fingers and neck too, you know? Like the type people get in prison."

I gulp and hope Kelly is okay. Her estranged grandfather sounds like a rough character who is not cut out to take care of a teenage girl.

26

IRENA

I pace the kitchen floor and say with each step, "Call me, Kelly. Call me." But my phone doesn't ring, and nothing new has been posted online by or about her. My phone dings with a social media notification, and I hurry to my laptop, opening a page online.

My eyebrows shoot up, and I stare at my screen. I lean closer to see better. "There you are, Kelly. Got you, sweet girl."

I call Violet with the news, and she picks up right away, saying, "Anything new? Have you seen Karina and Bernard?"

"No word from them since they set off in the snow. But I just found a text Kelly sent to my dad earlier today, asking him what he was doing. Maybe that kicked off his coming here and taking her while I was gone."

"I guess that's possible and makes sense, in a twisted kind of way. What else?"

"Her friend Plum told me," I start to say, but she interrupts me.

"Wait, did you say Plum is a kid's name? As in fruit?"

I shrug. "Sure, people are naming their kids all kinds of unusual names." She grunts, so I go on. "Plum says Kelly was supposed to be at her house at two, but she didn't show. She texted at three with one word, 'safe,' which is our code word for she's okay."

"This is getting stranger and stranger. Your daughter might've thought she was going willingly with her grandfather, who she barely knows. But he intends to take her and keep her."

I nod. "I think that sounds right. There's a small possibility she might've wanted to prove a point and get back at me for disappearing all day."

"Wait a minute, she could've gone to her dad's, couldn't she? This does not all rest on your shoulders, Irena. Speaking of that, have you called Jack yet to let him know she's gone?"

I groan and smack my forehead. "I forgot. How is that possible? I've got to let him and Abby know."

"Do that right after we talk, but first, tell me anything else you know, no matter how insignificant."

My heart races, and I let out a slow breath, trying to calm down. "The only other thing is I just checked online, and my father made the mistake of putting a photo online of him and Kelly. He tagged Kelly in the photo. It looks like they're in a mossy rain forest. Do you think they could be on the Washington coast? Maybe Forks or Hoquiam or Grays Harbor?"

She chuckles. "It rains so much in this area that they might be anywhere in Western Washington or Oregon." She's silent for a beat and adds, "The photo could be a trick and rigged to look like they're somewhere else. Next, you might see a photo of them by palm trees. I bet he's running for the Canadian border."

"If he was near the border in this weather, we'd see snow in the picture. You know, he might've learned how to alter photos in prison using photoshop or something like that to change the background."

"I agree. I'll see if Mimi can pinpoint their location from the post."

"Oh, I forgot to tell you, I found my dad's cell number when Kelly texted him."

I read it off to her, and she says, "Bingo, we're one step closer to finding them. Hang in there. We're working on it."

I cock my head. "Who is with you?"

"Mimi and Flora came in to help."

"On Christmas Eve? Tell them thank you. I appreciate it."

"We all love Kelly, and we want to bring her home."

I hang up, and my stomach growls, but I can't eat

while this is going on. I'm light-headed from all the stress, so I force myself to sit and drink water, staring out into the cold night. We're in a blizzard, working blind and grasping at straws for my daughter. Kelly could be anywhere.

27

KARINA

Bernard and I say goodbye to the older man in the plaid vest and clomp down his front steps. My feet are cold, but we've got to keep going. I point to a house across the street, where the interior lights blaze bright. "They have a clear view of Irena's place, so let's talk to them before calling my sister."

At the front door, Bernard knocks hard three times, making it sound like our mission is urgent, which is spot on. Christmas carols play inside, and I hum a holiday tune. Peeking inside, I see the entry is decorated with evergreen boughs and twinkling white fairy lights. I let out a sigh, because I was looking forward to celebrating our first family Christmas with Violet.

Bernard blows his nose on a white handkerchief. "Better ring the doorbell. They might be having a party and didn't hear us knock."

I ring the doorbell and picture sitting by a fire, warming my cold toes and sipping whiskey. We didn't get a chance to enjoy dinner. We gulped it down at Violet's office and rushed out. But food doesn't matter tonight. What matters is that we help find Kelly. I cringe as my imagination runs wild about her whereabouts and well-being. Her granddad could drive to Idaho or Montana and hide her in a remote cabin. If he switched cars, he could hide for years and no one would find them.

The door swings open and a rosy-cheeked redhead wearing a glittering silver tiara with rhinestones opens her arms. "Why are you out in this awful weather? Come in, come in. You must be cold."

A man with a red beret appears, pointing to the back of the house. "Yes, come in. Join us for a cup of cheer. Eggnog with rum? A glass of sherry, or a shot of whiskey?"

I exchange a look with Bernard and shrug. "Might as well, thanks." We follow the man into a kitchen where everything looks new and on trend, down to the white quartz countertops and an induction stove with brushed bronze handles. I eye the gorgeous appliance and let out a little sigh, wishing for a stove like that in my café.

The man smiles, gesturing to upholstered chairs around a live-edged long wooden table. "Take a seat. Tell us what you're doing out on this cold night. And what'll you have to drink?"

Bernard and I sit, and I pull off my winter coat. Sliding glass doors along the back of the house reflect light from a flickering gas fireplace in the kitchen. I rub my hands to warm them. "Thanks for inviting us in. I'd like a cup of hot water and a whiskey neat, please, if it's not too much trouble."

Bernard says, "I'll have the same, and thanks. It's awfully nice of you to invite strangers into your home on a night like this. The temperature is dropping, and the snow is deep."

While the man heats water and pours drinks, the woman tugs on her red blouse, where the buttons gap, and says with a wide smile, "No one's a stranger on Christmas Eve. What brings you here? Are you carolers going door-to-door?"

"Not really," I say. "We're friends with Irena from across the street. Her daughter Kelly disappeared with her grandfather today, and we're gathering information to help find her."

The man sets steaming mugs before us. Inhaling steam, I wrap my cold hands around a warm ceramic mug. My fingertips tingle with warmth. My toes begin to thaw in the warm kitchen. I sit back and sigh, wishing we were here under different circumstances.

The man crosses his arms, and his red sweater exposes long hairy arms. "I'm not sure why you're concerned. Her going with her grandpa should be fine, shouldn't it? She's with family on a holiday."

I set the mug down. "Except this is different."

Bernard nods. "He's been estranged from Irena for

over thirty years, and he has a mean streak that Irena experienced first-hand growing up. His nickname is Rattlesnake, for how fast he lashes out with his fists with little to no provocation."

The woman takes a glass of red wine and sits, pointing in the direction of Irena's house. "This wouldn't have happened if Kelly's mother had been home. That woman is gone far too often to be raising a child on her own."

I wince. "I'm sure she'd like to be home more, but she has a business to run."

"So do many of us," the man says with a frown, "but we manage to get home for dinner on time each night. Unlike some of our neighbors." He exchanges a glance with the woman.

I grip the table edge, and my stomach knots. "I don't think this is Irena's fault. She goes out in bad weather to save boaters' lives when distress calls come in and no one else is available. The Coast Guard depends on her to rescue boats before they run up on rocks. She's a hero in my book, considering what she does for work."

Bernard sets down his mug. "She responds to Mayday calls. Those don't always come at convenient times."

I pick up my glass and swirl the whiskey, inhaling the aroma. "Someone has to go rescue stranded boaters in the middle of the night."

The middle-aged woman twirls a strand of long red hair around her finger. "But it doesn't have to be her. Let someone else handle it, so she can be home. On many nights we've been woken up, hearing her car start, isn't that right, Russell?"

"That's right, dear. It happens all the time."

I push away from the table and stand, leaving the drink I no longer want. "We'd better get going."

Bernard tosses back his whiskey and stands by me. "Time is of the essence."

I shrug on my coat. "Did you happen to see Kelly come out of her house today?"

The two move closer together, and he says, "Don't know that we did."

She grins. "We were busy putting up decorations, and the weather made it extra special, being snug inside."

He pats her shoulder. "We're just two peas in a pod, aren't we?"

She sings, "Two buttercups in a flower patch."

He chimes in. "Two plums on a tree bearing fruit."

My eyebrows shoot up, and I clear my throat. "Did you see a man in his late sixties go into Irena's house?"

They shake their heads. "Nope."

Bernard tries again. "Did you see him leave and get in a gray sedan?"

The woman nods. "Yes, remember that, Russell? A man in a plaid flannel shirt and jeans came out of Irena's."

He claps his hands together. "We did see that, didn't we, dear heart?" He turns to us. "He brought her down the front steps arm in arm, like he was making sure she didn't get away."

I blow out a breath and wonder why it took so long for them to cough up this important piece of information. Bernard says, "This is important. What time did this happen?"

She puts a hand to her cheek and leans toward him. "That's tough one to answer. We started celebrating early. What do you think, Pookie Bear?"

He chuckles, and I clench my jaw. Getting information out of them is like using a scouring pad on a crusted-over pan. He says, "Well, Pookie-Poo, it was around the time we turned on the Christmas tree lights."

I say, "What time might that have been?"

They break into peals of laughter, and she says, "We have a holiday tradition of turning on the lights on the tree on Christmas Eve at precisely three-thirty in the afternoon."

He grins. "Because that's when we got married, at three-thirty in the afternoon. Wasn't San Francisco the best for our honeymoon?"

She leans into him. "It was." She says to us, "Stay a while, and we'll let you look through our five photo albums from our wedding and honeymoon. We had a marvelous time. You'll love looking at the photos. All our guests enjoy them."

I shudder because there's nothing worse than looking through someone else's photos. I tap a toe, wanting to report what we've learned to Irena and Violet. I say, "So, just to confirm, the time you saw Kelly with the man was at three-thirty this afternoon?"

They look at each other and laugh. "Yes."

Bernard says, "And they got into a gray sedan?"

He waves a hand across his face, as if this isn't a life and death matter. "Sure, that sounds right. Shall we break out the champagne, my love?"

She giggles. "Yes, it'll put me in the holiday spirit."

Bernard and I say goodbye, but they don't look our way, they're so taken with each other. I say in a loud voice, "If you remember anything else, please tell Irena."

Striding to the door, Bernard opens it, and I step outside, closing it until the lock snicks shut. Cold wind roars down the street, whistling in my ears. Snowflakes dance in the wind, and we tromp through the snow to Irena's house across the street.

When Bernard stumbles, I reach out to steady him. "Careful."

He huffs out a breath and glances back. "It was odd, how they reacted."

I nod as we approach Irena's house and say, "They were in a bubble, where bad news didn't reach them. They weren't concerned about Kelly, who lives right across the street."

"Maybe they hit the sauce hard and were tipsy."

I roll my eyes and groan. "Or, they're drunk on love and high on life."

"They're lucky to have each other." He sighs. "I miss your grandmother."

"I do too. Gigi's approach to problems was to bake scones, a café full of them."

He chuckles, as we stomp up Irena's front steps. Before I can knock, she swings the door open. Her eyes are wide, and she points to the living room with a trembling hand. "Come in. Tell me what you learned."

28

IRENA

Looking out the front window, I watch Karina and Bernard enter my neighbors' house across the street. I bite my lip and wait. As minutes tick by, I wonder why it's taking so long for them to ask a few simple questions when every minute matters. I text Violet and ask for any news but she doesn't reply. I'm alone on an island of angst.

I gnaw on a fingernail until finally, the door across the street opens, and Karina and Bernard emerge. They slog through snow and make their way to my house. Bernard stumbles, and Karina steadies him.

I hurry to the door and fling it open before they can knock. "Come in. Tell me what you learned."

I don't bother to take their coats because I want to get down to business right away. My father is a master manipulator who knows how to instantly turn into a charmer and make everyone like him, but my mother and I saw through his act, having lived with him. I wanted a puppy back then, but Mom said it wouldn't be safe with Dad in the house. Now my daughter is alone with a dangerous criminal who we didn't trust to be under the same roof with a dog.

I gesture to the living room and perch on the sofa, clenching my fists. "Let's call Violet and tell her everything you learned. Even a small bit of seemingly insignificant information might lead to Kelly coming home."

Bernard leans forward in a chair. Karina pulls out her phone, calling her sister.

I tap a toe, wanting to get this over with and give my daughter the biggest hug she's ever had. Tears prick my eyes, and I wipe them away with the back of my hand. Weeping won't help. There will be time for that later.

29

KARINA

My sister picks up on the first ring. "Any news?"

I grip the phone tight. "Bernard and I learned some things from the neighbors. We're with Irena at her place."

"I'll put you on speaker, so Mimi and Flora can listen in. Okay, what did the neighbors say?"

I nod to Bernard, and he says, "Irena's Dad's car appears to be light gray, according to one person."

I chime in. "They said he went in the house carrying a guitar case."

Irena slaps her knee. "She wants to play guitar. He could've used that as a bargaining chip, to get her to trust him."

"When they left," Bernard says, "it looked like he was keeping Kelly close and maybe forcing her to come with him down the steps."

Irena speaks up. "But Kelly texted a friend to say she was safe before they left."

Violet says, "It's possible the tone of things went sour after she sent that, and he turned hostile, forcing her out the door and into the car."

I look at Irena. "Your dad asked a neighbor for chains for his tires. It sounded like he was heading for a mountain pass. And according to the wacky neighbors across the street, Kelly and your dad left here at precisely three-thirty this afternoon."

Irena's mouth falls open. "Those two screw balls? All they do is stare into each other's eyes and talk about how they love each other so much. I don't know how they get any work done."

I tilt my head. "I thought it was sweet."

Bernard opens his hands. "They're quite sure Kelly was taken at three-thirty. The time has special significance for them because they were married then."

Irena groans, rolling her eyes. "Every day is a celebration of love with those two. How nauseating."

Violet says, "Don't let your breakup with Buzz color our investigation. We've all had sour grapes in love at some point. We'll accept what your neighbors said at face value for the time being, and the good news is we now have bread crumbs to follow on the trail to Kelly. I'll call and update the FBI agents with this information."

Irena stifles a sob. "I just want her to come home."

30

KELLY

I frown at my grandfather as he inches the car forward to the border crossing. We were stopped on the freeway by a rock slide that covered one lane, and we've been waiting in line for hours to cross into Canada. "I want to go home. Mom must be worried about me. Please, let me use your phone to call her."

"Shush," he says, turning and glaring at me. I wince when I see the long scar running from his left eyebrow down to his chin.

He says in a low voice, "We're almost at the border. Remember, keep your trap shut, and I'll do all the talking. Don't pipe up and say I took you, or I'll head right back to your house and hurt your mom. Zipped lips will keep your mother safe."

I look out the side window and wipe tears from my face. Whining and pleading hasn't worked with Granddad. He won't let me get out of the car. He won't turn around. He won't let me call Mom, who I'm sure must be frantic and out of her mind by now.

The car ahead of us at the guard shed drives across the border, and a green light comes on. Granddad pulls up to the border crossing guard shed and stops. A tall Black woman in a blue parka comes out. I gulp and consider telling her the truth, but I don't want my mom to get hurt. From the way he said it, with his dark eyes glinting and a slight smile, I think he meant it.

Granddad reaches over, grabs my hand and squeezes so hard I almost yelp. He whispers, "Remember what I said."

The guard bends over and look in the car. "What's your destination? Are you here for business or pleasure?"

I swallow and try to signal that something is wrong, but no words come out.

Granddad chuckles. "We're on vacation, heading to Alaska. I've always wanted to go there. We'll catch the ferry from Prince Rupert to Ketchikan and have the time of our lives."

She leans in and studies me. I give her a little wave with my right hand, while my grandfather clutches my left one. He's facing her, so I mouth the word 'help,' but I'm too late, and she's looked away. Turning her attention to Granddad, she says, "Guess you didn't hear, but the Prince Rupert route is down for required upgrades. You should've checked ahead."

Granddad pulls his hand from mine and drums his fingers on the steering wheel. The border guard watches him fidget and says, "Bellingham is the better route for you. It's not far. You can board the Alaska state ferry there, with no need to cross the border."

He clears his throat and frowns. I clench my teeth. Earlier today, he came over with a guitar as a gift for me. He said if I got in his car, I'd get another gift, so I went with him. How dumb was that? As soon as I climbed in his car, he locked the doors and drove off. Mom will be furious that I let him in the house and fell for his tricks. He's not the nice granddad I wanted, not at all.

He shrugs. "I thought it would be an adventure to drive into Canada to get on the ferry. Guess I didn't do my research well enough."

The guard peers at me, cocking her head. "And who are you?"

I purse my lips and look down. To keep my mom safe, I'll stay silent. He taps on my left hand, and I bite my lower lip.

He says in a gruff voice, "This is my granddaughter. She's not much for talking."

"Papers please."

He looks over at me. "Go on, get out your school ID and pass it over."

I try to act casual. "I left it at home when you told me to leave my phone."

The guard narrows her eyes. "Why did you tell her to leave her phone at home?"

He waves a hand. "Kids these days are always on their devices. I wanted to give her a chance to see the great outdoors without distractions."

She nods. "We can't let you through without identification."

He opens his wallet and pulls out a driver's license. "I have mine, and I'll vouch for her. She's my granddaughter, my own flesh and blood."

The woman points to a parking area that was cleared of snow. "Turn around there and go back. We can't allow you to enter Canada."

His jaw tightens. "Why don't we work something out? She's my granddaughter and just forgot it is all. I have my papers."

She crosses her arms, shaking her head. "There are no exceptions. Turn around over there. Do not proceed into Canada, or we will stop you and turn you into the authorities. You'll be arrested."

I rest a hand on my churning stomach. I don't want to be arrested.

His face flushes. "Okay, I get it. No need to threaten me. I've had enough of your unfair treatment."

She leans in. "Are you threatening me? Because if you are, I'll report it."

He waves a hand. "Forget about it. We'll be on our way."

He drives into the parking area and pulls to a sudden stop, making my head snap forward and whip back. He leans in, glaring at me. I swallow and tell myself I'll get home. Mom will find me. She'll track me down and rescue me.

Body odor wafts off his flannel shirt. His knee bobs up and down. The border guard's mention of the authorities hauling us in if we enter Canada really rattled him.

He hisses. "What're you up to, missy? Screwing with my hard-earned plans."

I shiver and shift to the far side of the seat. "I just forgot. It's no big deal."

He sticks a finger in my face. "No big deal, my foot. Watch your step or you'll be sorry. Don't screw this up. I've got a lot riding on this."

I slide my hand over to open the door, but find it's still locked. I lunge my arm over him to click open the doors, but he grabs me, shoving me back in my seat.

He slams a clenched fist down on the dashboard. "Do you hear me? Say yes, if you do."

My body is shaking, and my shoulders and arm hurt where he grabbed me. I wince and rub my left wrist. My throat tightens with tears, but I manage to say in a quiet voice, "Yes."

Spit flies out of his mouth as he yells, "Speak up. I can't hear you."

I take a deep breath and shout at the top of my lungs. "Yes."

"That's more like it. I can't stand people who go around cowering like timid little mice. It makes me want to hit them." He slams a hand on the steering wheel and drives off, heading back into the U.S. and flying over speed bumps.

Tears trickle down my cheeks and I wonder if I'll ever see my mom again. Stifling a sob, I cross my arms and blame myself. Mom warned me not to see her father because of his terrible temper and how he lashed out, but I didn't believe her. I thought he'd be kind, like grandfathers are in movies. This is my fault. I let a monster in the house.

He reaches over and pinches my left arm. "Buck up, and don't be a sad sack. No Debbie downers in my car."

A sob escapes from my lips, and I rub my stinging arm. "I want to go home. I miss my mom."

"Forget about her. We're going away, where you'll have a good time. If I have to punish you to make you smile, I will. I have no problem with that. That's why I have a whip in the back, to keep people in line."

I stare out the window at fields covered with snow and make a wish to find a way home. Come rescue me, Mom. That's what you do best. Find me. I should've listened to you. I'm sorry. I was wrong to send that text.

31

VIOLET

I call FBI Special Agents Frankie McNalley and Mark Brick and relay what we learned from Irena's neighbors. "Now we know when Kelly left the house and that she reached out to him by text before he came over. That muddies the waters a bit, doesn't it?"

Frankie says, "Although she initiated contact and he's her blood relative, the detail about her being made to get in a car makes me convinced this is a kidnapping."

Her partner, Mark Brick, speaks up. "I alerted the border guards. We'll see what they come up with."

Mimi and Flora enter my office. I nod to them and point to chairs, indicating they should sit down. "Mimi and Flora from my team are here too. I'll put you on speaker. Can you check cameras along the freeway for a light gray sedan heading north from Mt. Vernon to the Peace Arch at the Canadian border?"

Brick coughs. "That's like searching for a grain of sand."

Frankie says, "It is, and we're taking a look. What else have you got for us?"

I frown. "Irena told me her father has a temper, and he's got a scar on his face running from his left eyebrow to his chin. His nickname is Rattlesnake for how fast he lashes out with his fists with little or no provocation."

Mark says, "The guy's got a rap sheet, that's for sure. Our guess is the situation will deteriorate the longer Kelly is with him. Probably by now, she's seeing the real grandpa come out."

Frankie chimes in. "The not-so-nice granddad, who took a thirteen-year-old-girl from her home."

Mark says in a tense voice, "Hold on, I just heard back from Canadian Customs. They turned away a man matching our description with a passenger who might've been Kelly minutes ago. Granddad was trying to enter Canada and said they were driving to Prince Rupert to catch the Alaska state ferry, but that route is closed for the time being. It would've been faster for him to take the ferry from Bellingham, not far from the border crossing."

Frankie speaks up. "I bet he wanted to take her out of the country and disappear before we caught him. Maybe Alaska was a ruse used to divert our attention."

I tap a finger on the desk and glance at Mimi and Flora, who are sitting wide-eyed. "So, the question now is, where's Granddad going with Kelly next?"

Mimi leans forward. "If I were him, I'd get off the freeway, driving on roads that have been plowed."

I glance outside, where snow is still falling and accumulating on window sills and roof tops of other commercial buildings downtown.

Flora says in her high-pitched voice, "If it was me, I'd drive all night instead of stopping at a motel."

I blow out a breath. "If I were him, I'd head east of the mountains to a small town, somewhere like Republic or Omak, and hide out. I'd switch cars first in a metropolitan area."

Frankie says, "Eastern Washington is a long ways to go in a snowstorm, and he doesn't have a car for going through deep snow."

I clear my throat and lean in. "Unless he found some snow chains. But I think you're right. The prison he was in is over there, so I doubt he'd return to that area, due to bad memories and all that. But he might head south."

Mimi nods. "He could blend in on I-5 with other vehicles foolish enough to be out in a storm and make it to Oregon, hiding out there."

Mark says, "My bet is he'll hide out on the Washington coast, somewhere like Grays Harbor, where he might blend in."

"Or," Frankie says, "in a little town in Oregon, off the grid."

I gulp a quick slug of stale coffee. "He might break into a vacation cabin, while the owners are gone. My guess is he wants to get away and hide to start a new life with his granddaughter."

My throat tightens with fear for Kelly, and I break into a coughing fit. Mimi comes over and claps me on the back.

Frankie asks, "Everything okay over there?"

I shrug. "Sort of. I'm worried about Kelly."

"We are too," Mark says. "It's a shame we missed them at the border."

Frankie says, "Keep in touch."

"Will do." I hang up and rest my head in my hands.

Flora's high-pitched voice interrupts my dark thoughts. "What's next, boss?"

32

KELLY

Grandfather merges onto the freeway and accelerates. He frowns and taps his left hand on his thigh, mumbling to himself. I can't make out the words, so I say, "Where are we going?"

He looks over at me, and his eyes open wide, as if he forgot I was here in the car. "What? Oh, nothing, just making a plan. It's always good to figure things out ahead of time. No knee-jerk reactions for us Pickles, right, Irena?"

I tilt my head and narrow my eyes. "I'm not Irena, I'm Kelly."

His head jerks back, and he stares ahead. 'Right, right. Got to make a plan."

His jacket is on the seat between us, so while he focuses on driving, I slowly reach over and slip a hand into his pocket, looking for a phone. I feel the hard edge of a cell phone and pull it toward me with as little movement as possible.

I yelp when he grabs my wrist.

He says in a booming voice, "What're you doing?"

"Nothing. Just looking for a tissue."

"That's B.S. if I ever heard it. I'm starting not to trust you, Rene."

I rub my wrist and lean forward in the seat. "I'm not my mom. I'm Kelly. I'm your granddaughter"

He flinches. "Just shut up while I concentrate on driving."

The car skids in the snow, and my stomach knots. He hunches over the wheel and corrects course. I say, "Where are we going?"

He slams a fist on the steering wheel. "That's enough. Keep quiet until I say you can talk."

I wrinkle my nose at his rancid body odor and slide over in my seat, so I'm up against the passenger door. Now he'll have a more difficult time grabbing and hurting me with his hands. My parents divorced when I was young, but my childhood was paradise compared to what my mom's must have been like with this stinking mean man.

He leans forward and opens his mouth, letting out a loud burp. The car fills with a horrible odor of rotten hamburger. I breathe through my mouth and cringe, turning away.

He shifts to his left and lets out a fart. Wrinkling my nose and wincing, I throw an arm over my face and breath through my mouth. I push on a button to open the window, but the control doesn't work.

Gagging and gasping, I say, "Open the window, or I'll throw up all over you."

He presses a switch on the arm rest and lowers the window an inch. I stick my nose near the gap. "That's not enough. Lower it more."

"Kids are a pain in the butt. You'd better behave is all I can say."

The window comes down a third of the way, enough so wind rushes in, fluttering against my face, but not enough for me to climb out.

He says in a gravelly voice, "Don't even think about jumping. You're not that skinny, although you might be in a few weeks."

I swallow, and my throat is dry. I've got to escape from this car.

33

IRENA

I thank Karina and Bernard for their efforts and wave goodbye as they leave for Violet's office to see if they can help there. Hurrying to my laptop, I check for new posts on social media by my father or Kelly and release a sigh, sitting back with my hands dangling down. The wooden chair creaks and groans. I'm lost without my daughter and utterly useless. I'm no help at all. We'll be lucky to find her, because she could be anywhere by now.

I pick up my phone and call Violet. When she picks up, I say, "I know I have to stay home, but I've got to do something. I can't sit here twiddling my thumbs. What can I do to help?"

"You know your dad better than the rest of us. Where do you think he'd go, after being turned away from the Canadian border?"

I stand and tap a finger on my lips. "I bet he's dropped the idea of going to Alaska. He won't try to fly with her. He knows he'd be caught if he tried to take Kelly through an airport, and he doesn't have enough money to charter a private plane."

Violet says, "But remember the barefoot bandit a few years back? He stole small private planes. Would your dad do that?"

I nod slowly. "Nothing is out of bounds for him. He thinks he can do anything, so he might try to steal a small plane. As far as I know, he doesn't know how to fly. But he might've researched how to do it when he was in prison."

"He could have. I'll ask the FBI to call the warden and have them look into his search history. What else? Tell me all your guesses. We need to find Kelly and bring her home as soon as possible."

A shiver runs up my spine. "I don't think he'd go to Eastern Washington in this bad weather. The passes will be treacherous in the storm and might be closed."

Violet says, "Mimi just told me Stevens and Snoqualmie Passes are closed, forcing him to stay on the west side of the state or head south to Oregon. He doesn't have snow tires, chains or traction devices that we know of, because he asked one of your neighbors to borrow them before he was rebuffed. The Siskiyou Pass in Oregon is requiring traction devices, so cars won't get stuck, but he could drive along the Oregon coast to California."

I squint outside at a raccoon making tracks across

fresh fallen snow and tap on the window glass. It stops and stares at me before moving on. The creature has been living under my shed, and I haven't had the heart to call an exterminator. Before this night ends, I suspect we'll both be out in the cold, fighting for our lives and loved ones.

Violet says, "Irena, are you there?"

"Yeah, I'm here, but I wish it was under different circumstances. I'd like to crawl in a hole and hide, but I can't do that, can I? The situation feels hopeless, with such a huge area to search for her. I don't know how to narrow it down."

"Give me a few more minutes and try to concentrate. Where would your dad go?"

I chew on a fingernail, pondering the question. "It's been years since I knew him well, but when I was young, he talked about how he wished he lived on Columbia River. He wanted us to move to a tiny town in Skamania County and fish for our food. My mom refused. She wanted to stay where there were more people."

I wipe tears from my eyes, recalling how my father slapped my mom when she said she didn't want to move to a shack without heat and live off the land and from what he caught fishing. He screamed at her while I cowered in my room. If I could escape outside, I climbed my favorite tree and hid, shaking and shivering up high in the branches, with only the wind to soothe my rattled, tormented soul.

She interrupts my thoughts by saying, "So it was on the Washington State side of the river that he wanted to live?"

I whoosh out a breath. "Yes, but it feels like we're grasping at straws and don't have anything solid to go on. I don't even know what Kelly was wearing when she left the house."

Violet says in a calm, steady voice, "Don't worry, we've got this. Karina learned what she was wearing from your love bird neighbors. She was wearing a blue hoodie sweatshirt, blue plaid flannel pajama pants and sheepskin slippers."

I break down crying. "If I was a better mother, I'd know that."

"Listen, you did nothing wrong. This is not your fault. A good grandfather doesn't abduct his granddaughter, and we won't stop until we find him. We have his license plate from when he was turned back at the border. We're gaining on him in baby steps, but we'll get there. Trust us. Trust the FBI. The agents know Kelly and care about her. We all want her back safe and sound."

I release a ragged sigh. "Thanks. I don't know how I can repay you for all this."

"Don't worry about it. We love Kelly. Besides, you already owe me skipper lessons when I buy a boat."

I chuckle. "That's right. I forgot."

"Well, I didn't. Look, we'll work all night and tomorrow too, and we'll keep going. We won't stop until she's home. Now go eat something and rest. I'll call if anything comes up."

I hang up, feeling full of hope and heartened that the FBI and a team of experts are working on finding Kelly. Maybe we'll get through this long night, and Kelly will come home after all.

34

KELLY

Granddad rolls up the window, but the air still stinks. I want to tell him what he did was disgusting, but I'll save my energy for when we stop. I'll run away as soon as I get out of the car. Maybe I can leave a note for someone to find in a bathroom, showing my name, my mom's phone number and asking for help. I lean over and open the glove compartment, looking for a pen and paper.

He says in a loud voice, startling me, "Whoa, missy. Close that right now."

I rummage around, and my fingers touch cold metal in the shape of a gun.

He steps on the brakes, and the car in back of us on the freeway honks the horn. Leaning over, he slams the glove box shut. "I said leave it alone. You better start doing what I say, or I'll teach you the hard way."

"Why did you bring me along if you're going to be mean? You could've gone by yourself."

Flecks of spit fly from his mouth when he says, "I need you to do chores, like laundry, baking, cooking and washing dishes. I don't do scut work like that."

I reach over, pinching his arm. "Take me home now! I want my mother." I scream at the top of my lungs, which I now realize I should have done at the border. That was my chance, and I missed it.

He glares at me, the scar blazing an angry red, and the car swerves. A horn honks, and he looks back at the road, moving the wheel and correcting course, as my mom would say.

"You'll pay for that missy, when we stop. I'll teach you a lesson."

"No, you won't, because I'll get away. You can't keep me here with you. My mom and her friends and the FBI will find me. You'll be locked up in jail before you know it."

His eyes grow wide. "Why'd you mention the FBI?"

I cross my arms. "My mom knows two FBI agents. They'll catch you and put you in prison for kidnapping."

"You've got the wrong idea. This isn't kidnapping. This is a family outing. We're going on a permanent vacation. It'll be fun living along the river."

I shake my head. "Leave me at the next rest area, before you get in more trouble. Your parole officer wouldn't be happy to know what you're doing, would they?"

"I'm not letting you out of my sight. I made a plan, and I'm sticking to it. We'll live in a cabin by a river, and you'll do the chores while I fish for dinner."

I point to a sign on I-5 for a rest stop one mile ahead. "Stop there. I need to use the bathroom."

He grunts. "Nope, you're not fooling me."

I moan and rest a hand on my stomach. "I've got to go. You need to stop."

But he drives past the turn off for the rest area, and I swallow bitter tears. I'm in more trouble than I realized. I've got to find a way out of this mess.

35

JACKLYN

I cock my head and study my son, wondering if he is capable of changing his ways and stepping up to be a better person, like his father and I hoped. Rose and Max come in the dining room, interrupting our moment, and Dusty sighs, rubbing his right cheek where the fondue fork hit years ago.

Rose says, "What're you guys doing? How about we play board games?"

Dusty gazes at me with a slight scowl and shrugs. He seemed eager to start over when we were alone just now, but I'm unsure if he was sincere. He might have been using me on his chess board, playing a game to benefit himself. I'll have to be cautious and protect my heart, even if he is my flesh and blood. Christmas miracles do happen, but I doubt Dusty will turn on a dime and become a different, more generous version of himself suddenly on a cold night.

He says to his sister, "I guess. Okay."

Max raises his arms and shouts, "Monopoly!"

Rose shakes her head. "That game takes too long. How about something else? Mom, what do you have?"

I let out a long sigh. "I don't have any board games."

Rose's eyes grow wide. "You used to have so many."

I give my two grown children a long look. "That was before you two sent me to Shore Lodge, and my belongings were tossed in a dumpster."

Rose puts a hand to her forehead. "Of course, I'm so sorry, Mom."

Dusty has a hint of a smile before covering his mouth with his hand and coughing.

I blink back tears as memories come flooding back of how he abandoned Buddy at the shelter and admitted me to a secure facility. I have valid reasons to harden my heart like a stone against my son. It'll take more than a moment of remorse from him, which I haven't witnessed yet, for me to let him back in my life.

My dog trots in the room and sits, staring up at me, as if sensing something is wrong. When my husband died, Buddy and I became a two-pack, and my pup was all I had, because my kids were busy with their own lives.

I bend over and rub his soft ears. "What a sweet dog, yes, you are." He leans into me, and I sigh, feeling my tense back muscles begin to relax. "You are a bundle of love."

Max tilts his head. "Grandma's using baby talk with Buddy."

I smile at my grandson. "He likes it." I ruffle Max's mop of hair and wrap him in a great big hug. "I've got you now. I'm the Grandma Monster of Love."

Max giggles and hugs me before wriggling away. He says to his mom, "Can I stay up late? It's Christmas Eve."

Rose folds her arms. "I suppose we could put it off and make this a special night."

Dusty towers over her. "But I get my old bedroom."

She shakes her head. "Max and I are staying there. Find somewhere else to sleep. It's not your room anyway. You tried to sell Mom's house."

I put my hands on my hips and flick a glance at my son, reminded of their bickering when they were young.

He shrugs. "We'll play rock, paper, scissors for it."

She steps forward, poking a finger in his face. "But I claimed it first."

I step between them, separating them in a blast from the past. I don't need reminders of how they gave me headaches when they were young. "Don't argue, not while we have guests, and not in front of me. I've had enough friction in my life to last until I kick the bucket. Settle it outside with a snowball fight."

Max jumps in the air, issuing screams of delight.

Dusty eyes his sister. "I'm in, if you're game."

A gust of wind smacks the house, and snow swirls outside. Rose peers out the window. "I'd rather stay inside. The lights are on next door. How about I go ask if they have any board games we can borrow, just for tonight?"

Dusty pulls on his coat. "I'll go with you. It'd be good to get some fresh air." He adds in a low voice, "We need to talk about Mom and how she's doing."

Rose stops in her tracks and says in a quiet voice, "I won't side with you against her. Don't even try."

I nod to Rose as they leave and join my friends in the living room. Sitting by the fire, I push at a cuticle and worry about spending the night with my nemesis on the premises. If only he'd jump in his truck and drive away, but we're snowbound and forced to be in close proximity.

36

JACKLYN

Rose, Dusty and Max zip up their jackets and go outside. Thick snowflakes dance in the wind, and I stand at the door, calling, "Be careful."

Rose glances back and smiles, with Max by her side. Dusty bends and forms a snowball, tossing it at Rose. She grins. "Watch out, I'll get you for that." She throws a snowball at Dusty, and Max joins in, and snowballs are flying. One whizzes past my ears and smacks the door, and I close it, leaning back and breathing hard.

Bernice says from her spot by a blazing fire, "Pretty cold out, isn't it?"

I nod and sit by her. "It's wonderful to see them getting along, playing in snow."

Mary sits on the couch with Fred, "It's about time.

Those two have been at each other's throats since Dusty started to walk."

I nod. "It's been a competition between them, with so many imagined slights. But one snowball fight doesn't remake years of sibling rivalry. We'll need a major surgery to accomplish that." I gaze at the fire, and Mercury adds a log, winking at me. I add, "Which reminds me of plants."

Bernice chuckles. "And why am I not surprised to hear that?"

I smile and cross my legs, crisscross applesauce style, as my kids used to say. "It's like they're two types of apples, grafted onto the same branch. I'm thunderstruck at how they had the same starting point, but grew into completely different beings."

Mercury sits beside me, his brown eyes gazing into mine. "That's what families are like. One tree bearing many kinds of fruit, and you don't know what you'll get."

Mary leans in. "But is it nature or nurture? Or both?"

I shrug. "It's got to be a little of both, but my bet is on how they experience the world. There's so much a parent can't control, especially these days."

Bernice's friend stares at the fire. "You're spot on about that. Most parents don't know their kid is bullied at school."

I frown. "Maybe that's what happened to Dusty. I'll have to ask him."

Mary says, "It's a little late to revisit that, don't you think?"

Mercury gently bumps his shoulder against mine. "It's never too late for a mother to show concern. Maybe he'd appreciate it."

The door flings open wide, and snow flies inside. Cold air blows in, making me shiver, despite the fire's warmth. I jump up and say, "Come in and close the door. What happened next door?"

Max says, "I'm hungry."

Rose holds up her hands. "We came up dry. The woman there said all she had was a collectible version of Candy Lane, but she couldn't lend it out. It was too valuable."

Dusty closes the door with a thud. "She told me to come back for a night cap. Maybe I'll spend the night there."

Rose rolls her eyes. "Sorry to rain on your parade, but she was just being polite."

Mary jumps off the couch. "Who wants food? I'll rustle something up."

"I'll help," I say and start toward the kitchen, but something about the way Dusty is looking at me catches my attention. He's standing by the door tapping a finger to his lips, staring at me. His isn't a warm, loving gaze, but a cold, calculating one. Am I being paranoid because of how he tried to sell my house out from under me? Perhaps I am.

I shudder and vow to be watchful while he's under my

roof and not underestimate the evil my son can create. You're only innocent the first time around.

37

DUSTY

I catch myself staring at my mom and look away, but not before she catches me. I've got to be careful and not reveal my true motives. My best bet is to ingratiate myself, make her trust me and pounce on the opportunity to take back what is mine. I'll wear her down, like I did with Dad. The strategy worked, so I'm in it for the long haul. I want to build houses, like I did before Mom ripped it away.

I follow her into the kitchen. The counters are clean, the dinner and dessert dishes have been washed and put away, but there on the kitchen table is a big pecan pie, sitting untouched. My mouth waters, imagining biting into a gooey, sweet, nutty bite. I could eat the whole pie by myself, but I'll force myself to be polite and play the long game.

"Hey, Mom, I'll help. Want me to serve slices of pie to everyone?"

Mom tilts her head and blinks at me. I open my hands and say, "What, are you surprised I'm willing to help? I'm turning over a new leaf. Just watch and see. I'm a new man."

Mary and Bernice come in the kitchen, making it feel crowded. I can't help but scowl at Bernice for foiling my plans to sell Mom's home, but then I force a peaceful expression on my face with a fake half-smile. "Hello, Bernice."

She goes over to Mom and gives her a hug. "We're heading out."

Mom purses her lips. "So soon? It feels like you just got here."

Bernice motions to the living room. "We just started hanging out together, and I don't want to overwhelm her, like back up the U-Haul truck on the second date."

We chuckle at that, and she adds, "As always, it's been lovely, sitting by the fire on Christmas Eve. Let's get together soon."

Mom glances at me, and I pull a knife from a drawer to slice the pie. I cut the pecan pie into thin slices because we've got a lot of people packed in the house who will want pie. I hum to myself and take small plates from the cupboard.

Mom takes Bernice over to the sink and says in a low voice, "I didn't tell you yet, but the city is messing with my building permit by adding steps to the process. It's totally ticking me off."

They glance at me, and I shrug, sliding a piece of pie onto a plate. Clearing my throat, I say, "I could help you navigate that. Just ask, and I'll help."

Mom nods to me. "I'll think it over." She says to Bernice, "We'll talk later."

They hug, and Bernice strides out of the room. She calls, "Bye, Dusty."

"Bye," I say and in my mind, give her the finger for ruining my well thought out plans. She's enemy number one in my book, and I'll have to think of ways to screw her up, but right now, I'm focused on winning my mother over to achieve my ultimate goal. I can't be distracted by side issues and skirmishes of lesser importance. Get Mom to give me the company, then even the rest of the scores, starting with those who tripped me up, like Bernice and Fred.

I smile to myself and slide a piece of pecan pie onto a white plate. Tonight is the perfect opportunity to execute my plan.

38

JACKLYN

Mary and I bustle around in the kitchen making coffee and setting out cookies, while my son dishes up pie at the kitchen table. He glances at me a few times as he works, and hairs on the back of my neck stand on end. Wind barrels down, shaking the house and rattling window panes. A branch hits the roof and clatters to the ground. I look out the kitchen window at snow covering my flower beds, garden and lawn.

Mary takes drink orders and comes back in the kitchen.

I say, "What happened to the rainy Christmas we always have?"

She shrugs. "Guess we got lucky this year with a white Christmas."

Dusty clears his throat. "It gives us more time to spend together."

I bite my lower lip and swallow words better off not voiced. "Coffee?"

He says, "Sure, I'll take mine with amaretto, if you have it."

Mary grins. "Same for me."

I shake my head. "I don't have amaretto, but how about Bailey's?"

Mary nods. My son says, "Works for me. Would you like me to serve pie in the living room, or the dining room?"

His body language looks relaxed, and the knots in my back start to loosen. But then I notice his dark brown eyes are cold and flat, and I remind myself of who he was when I was most vulnerable as a recent widow. Fear sweeps over me, reminding me of when I fought for my life in frigid water after escaping from a secure ward on an island. He's acting kind, and I can't trust him. My husband bought into our son's twisted truth, but I won't.

"Mom?" Dusty says. "Earth to Mars. Are we eating pie in the dining room or on our laps in the living room?"

I force out a chuckle. Two can play at this game and pretend to be someone we aren't. I'll catch him off guard when he's least prepared and teach him a lesson in humility. "In the living room. We'll be cozy by the roaring fire."

Mercury pops in the kitchen, tugging on his mustache.

"We're running low on firewood and need more. Where do you keep it?"

"Outside, on the far side of the garage."

He tromps out, and wind whips inside before he closes the door with a thud. Dusty carries forks and napkins to the living room. I measure out ground coffee and dump it in the basket.

Mary leans over and says in a low voice, "He's trying to make peace with you. You know that, don't you?"

I nod and pour water in the coffee maker. "Sure, I've noticed, but he's pretending. It's an act. I bet he has more tricks up his sleeve, like he did after his dad died."

"I wouldn't be so sure about that. Maybe he's learned his lesson."

Dusty comes in the kitchen. "Shall I hand out slices of pie or would you like them to come to the kitchen and get them?"

Mary gazes at me and nods, as if proving her point.

Pressing the brew button on the coffee maker, I say, "Let's wait until Mercury comes in to pass out dessert."

The front door bangs open and slams shut. I trot out to see what's going on. Mercury pulls off a brown knit hat and shrugs out of his jacket, hanging it on a hook. "We're fresh out of firewood. We can light candles for atmosphere and rely on the furnace for warmth."

I put my hands on my hips. "But I bought firewood a few weeks ago."

Mercury opens his hands. "Maybe someone took it?"

"No one does that around here. It's a quiet neighborhood, where nothing ever happens."

Max jumps up from the dwindling fire, where coals are glowing red. "I'll light candles."

"We'll light one together, and I'll do the rest." I put a hand to my forehead. "What happened to the firewood I bought?"

I go over to the living room window and cock my head when I see smoke coming out of the chimney next door. But I'm sure my new neighbor wouldn't take my firewood. No one would stoop that low, would they?

Someone knocks hard on the door, and I flinch, hurrying over to peer out the peephole. Bernice and her friend are shivering on the front porch. I fling open the door and gesture inside. "Back so soon?"

Bernice comes in, stamping her feet, and her friend joins us. "It's cold out there, and my car got stuck in the snow. I'm afraid we'll be here all night. I hope that's okay with you?"

I swallow and wonder how it'll work with so many people cooped up together in a storm. I open my arms, giving her a hug. "You're welcome here anytime. Come in and make yourselves at home."

Fred stands from the sofa. "You can have my seat. If you couldn't drive out, we'll have to leave our car here and walk home."

Mary says, "We can't leave yet. Not before midnight."

Bernice points to the window. "Mary and Fred, there's

no way you're walking home in this tonight. It won't be safe. There's a layer of ice under the snow, and you could slip and fall."

Fred shrugs. "We'll be fine."

Mary goes over to him, tugging on his arm. "We're staying. Bernice is right."

He folds his arms and frowns, as a gust of wind batters the house. "Fine."

"I'll bring out more camp chairs," I say.

"I'll help you, Grandma," Max says. "Mom says you shouldn't work so hard."

I glance from him to Rose, who shoves her hands in her pockets and looks down, and I say, "Thanks, but I can handle it."

Rose touches my arm as we walk in my study. "Sorry, Mom. You don't need to be babied. Just don't push yourself too hard with this new building project. I worry about your health."

I kiss her cheek. "No need to worry about me. I'll be fine."

We walk in the study, followed by Max, and stop in our tracks.

My son is rummaging through my desk drawers and didn't hear us. He says to himself, "Now where would she have hidden her checkbook? And the papers where I signed over Stone Construction? I need to get my hands on those now."

I clear my throat, and he turns. His jaw drops, and he says, "What're you doing here?"

Max runs over, wraps his arms around my son's leg. "Surprise!"

I unfurl my clenched fists and want to scream, but I won't, not in front of my grandson. I force out a fake laugh. "What am I doing here? I live here. The question is why are you going through my papers? Just as I was thinking I might trust you again. Shame on you, Dusty. Go on, get out of my sight!"

"I was just checking to make sure your personal papers are safe. I care about you and want to protect you."

I cock my head and can't help but glance up at a heating vent in the ceiling above my desk. I look him directly in the eyes and say in a firm voice, "Give me a break. That's a load of crap if I ever heard it. The documents are stored away from prying eyes in a safe place. And right now it seems the only thief I'm in danger of having in my home is you."

Rose chimes in. "Yeah, Dusty, stay away from her stuff."

Dusty acts as if he's done nothing wrong. He says, "Watch out for identity theft and scammers when you're on your computer. They can get to you, if you're not careful."

I shake my head. "I'm not an idiot. I haven't had my head in the sand."

Rose touches my arm. "Mom, he's probably right. Just be careful."

I arch an eyebrow. "This reminds me of when you two ganged up on me before."

Max says, "What did they do?"

"They sent me to a retreat center that turned out to be a locked room."

Max looks up at me. "They sent you to that place on the island, Stony Lodge. I knew you wouldn't like it there."

"You were right. I didn't like it one bit."

Dusty waves a hand, as if it's no big deal. "But that's all in the past."

I frown. "It feels very real to me now, with you rummaging through my room. I can't trust you at all."

Buddy runs in, rolling around on his back on the rug. Dusty picks up Max and starts to carry him out of the room, but he stops and stares at the ceiling vent before leaving.

I frown at his back. He played me earlier, just as I suspected, by putting on a sincere façade and saying he wanted to talk things out. Forget having a jolly, relaxing holiday with friends and family. This is war.

39

DUSTY

I swing Max around Mom's study and look around one last time before she sends me packing from the room like a little boy. I bet she hid documents in the ceiling vent, which fits with her not being mentally capable. I'll find time later to slip away and see what's hidden in the vent when I'm alone.

Tucking Max under my arm, I carry him down the hall. "Zoom, you're an airplane, zoom, zoom."

I go in my old room and plop him down on the camp bed. "There you go buddy. See you later. I've got things to do. Got to help grandma, you know."

He opens one eye. "I don't believe that. She wasn't nice to you just now. Why is that?"

I ruffle his hair and tickle him in the armpits until he laughs. "Families don't always get along. But we love each other, even if we argue and get mad sometimes."

He sits up. "That's what my mom says."

I lean against the door jamb. "That's because she's my sister, and we grew up together."

He looks up at me. "But it doesn't seem like you even like each other."

I shrug, crossing my arms. "Well, we don't live near each other, so that makes a difference."

He stands and brushes off his pants, like Rose does. I scoop him up and twirl him around, giving him a great big bear hug. Setting him down, I say, "You be good, okay? Do whatever your mom says."

He gives me a half-smile. "Okay."

My sister walks in the room. "You two getting set up? We've got a lot of people staying over tonight."

Max says, "What happens at midnight? Why did Fred mention that?"

Wiggling my fingers, I say in a creepy voice, "That's when the boogey man comes out."

Max's eyes grow wide, and his lips tremble. Rose wraps her arms around him, glaring at me. "Don't scare him. Now he'll have nightmares."

I rest my hands on my hips. "Max, I was just kidding. Midnight is when Santa's reindeer come down on the roof. If you're lucky, you might get a gift tomorrow, like an orange or a candy cane."

Max brightens. "Or a Beamer One remote control monster truck?"

Rose taps a toe. "Don't get his hopes up. I won't be running errands in this weather."

40

KELLY

Granddad drives south on I-5 through snow, and windshield wipers whip back and forth, groaning with the motion. I can barely see through the fogged glass. He wipes a cloth over the windshield in front of him and hunches over, staring ahead and clutching the wheel. Flicking on the radio, he hums along to Christmas songs. I stare at a snow-covered car looming ahead of us in the right lane. It doesn't appear to be moving.

For a split second, I think of us crashing into the car, and an ambulance taking me away from this man and home to my mother. But I point and say in a loud voice, "Watch out."

He slams on the brakes, and the car skids, sliding sideways. My heart races, and I brace for impact, tensing every muscle, but we whisk past the other car, fishtailing into another lane. A car behind us lays on the horn.

Granddad growls. "Damn thing was parked on the freeway. Who does that? We could've been killed."

I say in a tight voice, "Mom says people near Seattle don't know how to drive in snow. Maybe they were afraid and panicked."

"That's no excuse." He turns off the radio and takes the next exit, sliding down the slight slope of the off-ramp and coming to a stop on the shoulder of the road. I spot a convenience store with the lights on about a half-mile away.

He sighs. "I'm tired. I'm going to take a nap."

My fingers curl into tight fists. I undo my seatbelt and try the door handle again, but nothing happens when I pull on it. "Granddad, I have to go to the bathroom. Let me out."

"You're not going anywhere. We'll find a fishing cabin and start over. It'll be a swell time. You'll like it, just you and me, girlie. I found my family again, and I won't let you go."

I blow out a slow breath to calm myself, like Mom taught me when my dad went missing. "I need to go to the bathroom, right now. I can't wait."

He grunts and turns off the car. Snow flies past, and a strong blast of wind makes the car shudder. I've got to find a way to jump out of the car and run to the store to get help.

His chin dips down to his chest, and he starts to snore.

I reach over him, my hands shaking, and unlock the car doors. While I'm at it, I take the key from the ignition, so he can't follow me.

"Huh?" He snorts and opens his eyes, looking around. "What're you doing? Give me back those keys."

He reaches out for me, but I'm too fast for him. I open the car door and tumble into the snow, landing on my butt. I jump up, throw the car keys as far as I can and stumble through the snow, running as fast as I can in my slippers.

Sweat trickles down my arms. My heart pounds, and my feet slip and slide. My slippers fall off, and every step is agony. I thought I was strong from taking dance lessons, but now I'm not so sure about that.

I climb an embankment to the road and glance back, breathing hard. He's jogging toward me on the slick, plowed road. I pick up my pace and run, slipping and sliding in bare feet. The store is only fifty feet away. I can make it.

I'm panting hard and soaked with sweat by the time I stumble into the store parking lot. I slip and fall, picking myself up. My knees hurt, my legs are shaking, and my lungs ache from sucking in cold air.

Approaching the store, I smile because I'm almost there. Soon, I'll be safe. But the outside lights blink off, and a neon sign in the front window goes dark. A thin man appears at the door, and I run toward him, waving my arms. "Help, help!"

He's wearing headphones and looking down, fiddling with the lock. He heads toward the back as I come to the door. I bang my fists against the glass, but he doesn't turn around. "Help!"

Lights inside the store click off, one by one.

I pound on the glass with my fists and scream for help.

The sound of a whip cracks behind me, and I flinch. Granddad must be close by.

He clears his throat. "Come back to the car with me, or I'll make you regret running away from me."

I smack on the door with my sweaty palms. "Open up!"

The whip snaps, lashing out at my back, and I gasp at the stinging white-hot pain. Quick as I can, I turn and reach down, grabbing the line from the ground and yanking the whip out of his hands. His jaw drops, his eyes grow wide, and the jagged scar on his face turns an angry red.

I coil the whip and stand with my hands on my hips. "You won't get away with this. They'll arrest you."

He scowls. "Stop playing games, princess. Let's get out of here. You'll like living by the river."

"No, I want to go home. You can't make me go with you."

He hisses, "The river calls."

He stretches out his arms and lunges for my neck, but I jerk away and run around the building to the back door. I turn the cold metal knob, but it's locked. Pounding my palms against the window in the door, I kick at the wood panel until my bare feet bleed and sting, but no one comes.

Granddad comes around the corner, leaning against the wall, breathing hard.

Squinting inside, I see the store lights are off, but a crack of light shines from under a backroom door, so maybe the man went in there. A big rock sits on the ground by the door, perhaps used to prop it open. I pick up the stone with trembling hands and bash it into a reinforced window in the rear store door. Glass shatters, falling to the ground.

An alarm goes off, blaring on a cold December night. The window glass is mostly gone but a grid of crisscrossed metal wires remain. I'll have to smash the wires to push my hand inside and open the door.

Tears stream down my cheeks, and I'm panting hard. I lift the rock from where it fell on the ground, smash it against metal wires in the window and scream. "Help. Call the police."

Gasping, I gulp for air and hear my grandfather wheezing, coming closer. Goosebumps prick my flesh. My bare feet are cut and bleeding, and I clench my jaw, pushing away the pain. My toes are turning numb from standing in snow.

My granddad shuffles toward me with heavy footsteps.

He doesn't look healthy, and his face is pale. We won't last long out in this cold.

I pound on the door with my fists, calling for help, but then recall what my mom said. I yell, "Fire!" But no one comes to the door, and the alarm shrieks with an ear-piercing wail.

I glance around the snow-filled parking lot, looking for a car. The man has to have a way to get home from here. My heart races, and I run to a pickup truck, pulling on the driver's door handle, but it's locked.

Granddad glares at me, stumbling through snow and moving toward me with his arms outstretched. It might look like a gesture of affection between some family members, but he looks ready to kill me.

His breath hangs in the cold night air when he says in a hoarse voice, "I've got you now, girlie. You won't get away."

A snow shovel leans against the store wall, and I shove the whip in the waist of my pants and run. Picking up the shovel, I wave it in the air. "Come any closer, and I'll hit you with this."

He laughs, tipping back his head, and lumbers toward me. "You won't get the better of me, lass. Hasn't your mother taught you that yet?"

I plant my near-frozen feet on the frigid ground and brandish the snow shovel in the air as a weapon. "I'm warning you. Don't come any closer."

41

IRENA

Gritting my teeth, I drum my fingers on the kitchen table and mull over what to do next. I've got to do something to bring Kelly home. Taking a chance I might see my dad's car on I-5, I check the Washington State Department of Transportation traffic cameras along the freeway online but don't see a gray sedan. Snow obscures my vision, making it difficult to see vehicles in the blizzard. It's all a blur.

An alert dings, and I check social media. Kelly's friend Plum posted, 'Has anyone seen Kelly? I think she went with her grandfather somewhere this afternoon. Call her mother if you've seen her. She doesn't know where Kelly is.'

Within minutes, people pile on the post with comments. 'Is this a joke?' And, 'I get it, it's a game, like where's Waldo.' An anonymous poster says, 'If she's with family, she's fine. Don't worry about her. Mind your own business.'

My eyes fill with tears, and I wipe them away, but I can't stop staring at the screen. Another person's post pops up. 'The mother is to blame. She should know where her daughter is. Where was she when this happened?'

The last post hits me hard, and I break into bitter tears. Finally, I sit back and release a shuddering sigh, saying in a tear-clogged tight voice, "They're right, this is all my fault. I should know where my daughter is."

I stand and blow my nose, tossing the tissue on the floor. I grab my phone and call Violet. I've got to do something to rescue Kelly from her grandfather's grip.

Violet picks up on the second ring, and I pace back and forth, saying, "Anything new on your end? Have you located his car?"

"We're looking everywhere but haven't found it yet. Images on traffic cams are hard to see in this weather."

I whoosh out a breath. "People are blaming me on social media."

"Uh huh. We saw that just now. I was hoping you wouldn't notice the nasty comments. Try to ignore them."

"It's too late for that, and I can only blame myself for what happened."

"Try to think of something else, and let us do our job, We need to focus on finding her."

I puff out a breath. "You're right. My calling you isn't helping. You guys need to work without distractions."

"Hold on, Mimi's got something."

I hear voices on the other end of the line and try to listen in but can't make out what they're saying. Violet comes back on the line. "We may have something, but it's tenuous at best. Don't get your hopes up."

I grip the phone. "What? What is it? Tell me."

"It might be nothing. It's too soon to know. Wait for the FBI to call you."

I stomp a foot on the floor. "I want to know everything that might have to do with Kelly, real or not."

"Fine. Police are responding to an alarm going off at a convenience store near I-5, and they're heading there now. A man who works there says a girl is screaming outside, and an older man is trying to take her away with him."

"I'll go see if it's her. Where is it?"

"We don't know for sure it's Kelly. It could be someone else."

"I need to help her. Tell me where they are."

"I shouldn't have mentioned it and gotten your hopes up. Sit tight, and I'll call you when we know for sure."

I say in a loud, clear voice, "Which town is it? Which store?"

"It wouldn't be right for me to tell you. Police are heading to the scene now."

She hangs up, and I throw my hands in the air before opening my laptop and searching for an ongoing incident at a convenience store off I-5. Finding nothing, I shake my head and mutter, "I knew Dad was dangerous but never guessed he'd go this far."

An idea occurs to me, and I post on social media, saying if anyone knows about an incident going on in Western Washington near I-5 with a girl at a convenience store, to let me know where it's happening.

I stand up and start pacing the kitchen floor. The wall clock ticks as seconds slowly pass, but my pulse pounds in my ears. We've got to stop my father before Kelly disappears forever.

42

DUSTY

While everyone gathers in the living room, hanging out by a dying fire, I jump on my chance to sneak back into Mom's study. I tiptoe down the hall and enter the room, letting a smile spread across my face. She thinks she can outsmart me by hiding precious papers, but I'll show her.

I take a dime from my pocket and raise my arms, loosening some of the screws holding the metal ceiling vent in place. Warm air from the furnace blows in my face, and I sneeze from inhaling dust. One of the screws is stuck, and I glance around the room. Grabbing my dad's rolling office chair, I push it under the vent and kneel on it to get more purchase. I reach up and push on the stubborn screw, but the chair scoots out from under me. I land on my back, flat on a fancy rug Mom bought after I did her a favor and cleared out her place.

I groan and roll on my side.

Mom comes in the study and cocks her head, studying me on the floor. "Need some help?"

I clench my jaw and get up off the floor. "I'm fine."

She crosses her arms. "We're both fine and looking out for ourselves, aren't we?"

I rest a hand on my aching back, which was injured when I fell off a ladder on a job site, and say, "Whatever. You're always right, in your mind."

She glares at me, her blazing blue eyes boring a hole into my heart, exposing my vulnerabilities and wounded feelings. I stumble out the door, blinking back tears as I head down the hall to the kitchen, and frown when I see someone stole my piece of pecan pie that I set aside on the counter.

Max runs up to me with Buddy by his side. "I had two pieces of pie. It was really good."

I pretend to be stern with him. "You ate my pie, so now I'll gobble you up."

I growl and reach for him, and he squeals, running down the hall with the dog in his wake. I lumber after him and let out a sigh. What I wouldn't give to have a home like this and a family of my own and my old life back, but my mother ripped my possibilities away.

When I follow Max into the study, Mom looks over from her desk. "Go on, find somewhere else to play, you two." She points to the hall. "Anywhere but here."

I glance up at the ceiling, eyeing the vent. I've got to

get time alone in this room tonight to see what she hid inside the vent. Mom and I lock eyes, and a shiver runs through me.

Max and Buddy trot out of the study, and I lean against the wall in the hall, crossing my arms and watching my mother come out and close the door, locking it. She puts the key in her pants pocket and pats it before walking up to me.

"Dusty."

"Mom."

We eye each other in the tight space. There's barely room for two of us to stand. Recalling she has claustrophobia, I pull myself to my full height and lean over, trying to tower over her, so she'll cower. But she just steps by and shrugs.

As she walks away, I say, "Why'd you lock it? You never do that."

"Tonight is different. I have people under my roof who I'd rather not have meddling with papers in my study."

I tilt my head. "But we need space for people to sleep. Without the study, we'll be too crowded with everyone staying over and snowed in."

She comes back and pats my shoulder, like she did when I was young, and I bristle inside. She may think it's a loving gesture, but I find it condescending.

She says, "It's not your concern. I'm in charge, and this is my house."

I follow her around for a while, hoping to see where

she might put the key to the study, but she just pats her pocket from time to time and doesn't stop gabbing with her friends in the living room.

I slink back into my old room and sink onto the floor, resting my head in my hands. My whole world was turned upside down when Dad died. I get an idea and pull off my boots, setting them aside and walking softly down the hall toward the study. A floor board creaks, and I freeze in place, heart thudding.

When no one comes, I hurry the last few steps and stop by the study door. I pull out my phone, use the flashlight app and inspect the door knob. When I was growing up, and Rose locked herself in the bathroom after we had a fight. She was weeping and wailing on the other side of the door, and my dad who was home at the time, like he often was compared to Mom. He showed me how to open the door. He was good with tools and encouraged me, not like Mom, who was obsessed with their garden store.

I frown. Who cares about another begonia? What about your son, pining away for love at home while you're working?

Voices murmur in the living room, and I nod to myself. I'll find a tool and, when everyone is asleep. pop this baby open, slip in the study and get inside the ceiling vent. And if I'm lucky, I'll find her checkbook tucked in a file cabinet. I'll rip out two or three checks for my use and forge her signature.

The hall overhead light flicks on, and I flinch.

Mom clears her throat. "Just what are you up to?"

I cringe, caught red-handed, like when I was little. She could always sense when I was up to no good, except for after Dad died. "Nothing much."

She pulls out the key, dangling it in the air. I can't help but stare at it. I'd love to grab it and barge into the room to find whatever she's hiding, but I whistle and look up at the ceiling.

She smiles. "Bet you'd like to have this, wouldn't you? But that won't be happening, not tonight or on any other night. Just forget it."

A pang of grief stabs my chest, and I bend over. I must not cry in front of her. A few lines of a fresh poem run through my mind: 'Wounded when a mother's love is cast aside, he wept for days, struck down in his youth, unable to advance.'

I slap a hand on the wall for support. "I don't know what you're talking about."

Stumbling into my old bedroom, I pull on my boots, shrug on my jacket and slap a hat on my head. I weave my way through the pack of partygoers in the living room and reach for the door knob.

Behind me, Mom says, "Where're you going?"

"Just out for a smoke."

"If you see any firewood," Mercury says, "bring it back with you. I didn't see any when I was out there."

43

JACKLYN

As I put on my jacket to follow my son outside, Mary says, "Where are you going?"

Zipping up my coat, I pull on my black knit hat. "To check on the firewood situation. I bought a bunch of it before, but now it's missing, which frosts me mightily."

She stands. "I'll go with you."

I wave her off, wanting to creep around quietly to see what my son is up to outside. He had a gleam in his eyes that I recognize from when he was young and up to mischief. "No need for you to come. I'll be fine."

Bernice leans back, letting out a hearty laugh. "That's Jacklyn's motto. I'll be fine on my own."

Mary nods. "And an admirable one. Until it gets in your way. Always good to have help now and then, right, Jacklyn?"

I roll my eyes and flap my arms. "I'm getting hot in here. Are you done roasting me, so I can leave?"

Bernice and Mary motion to the door, and Bernice's friend says, "Give us the weather report when you come back."

I open the door, and a blast of frigid air blows in. Everyone shudders and shivers, rubbing their arms. "Sorry about that," I say, closing the door as quietly as I can.

I stop and listen on the front porch, hearing movement in the garage. Trees sway and moan in gale force winds. Snow swirls in the storm, and I blink as snowflakes blow into my eyes. My fingers grow cold, and I shove them in my pockets. This is not a night to be out, but I feel driven to follow my son and see what he's doing. He's certainly not having a smoke, like he said he would.

I stand on the snowy pavement and peer in the garage window. Dusty is opening drawers in his dad's workbench and slamming the drawers shut. He kicks one back in place and misses, hitting his shin on the wood and hopping in place, cussing.

He glances over, and I duck down. He must be looking for a tool to get into my study. My heart skips a beat when I realize he might find what he's looking for in the garage, because that's where I keep my shrine to how I escaped from Shore Lodge. One Philips' head screwdriver was all it took to open the gate to my freedom that night. When I got home and set up my house, I bought a collection, the best I could find, of those special screwdrivers that saved my sanity.

I put my hands around my eyes to see better and watch my son wander around my garage. He finds my screwdrivers and grabs two of them, juggling them in the air. He crouches low and brandishes the screwdrivers like weapons, pretending he's having a sword fight or a duel.

I nod to myself, because he always loved pretend sword fights as a child.

Someone clears their throat close by, and hairs on the back of my neck stand on end. I whip around, my heart racing, and face the new neighbor next door. Zoila is wearing a long flowing blue velvet robe with the hood up over her dark hair and knee-high black boots. Resting my hand on my heart, I say, "You scared me, sneaking up like that."

She breaks into a smile. "I wasn't sneaking around. You were hiding. What're you doing out on a night like this?"

I glance at the garage window, and she says, "Can I look too?"

I put a hand to my forehead and wish I hadn't come out to skulk around when I have guests to entertain. What kind of mother follows her son and waits to pounce when he does something wrong? I gesture to the window. "Have at it."

Dusty comes to the window and waves, grinning at my new neighbor. I frown because I opened the door, and now I bet he'll be over all the time to see her, while trying to wriggle his way back into my life.

Dusty says, "I'll come out and join you."

I glance at the spot where I left a stack of firewood by the garage and say to my neighbor, "My firewood is missing. Might you know where it went?"

Zoila rubs her long fingers together and grins. "It was just about on my property, so I moved it. I'm using it now and having a fire. Want to come over?"

I ball my hands into tight fists and bite back words I might regret later. "No, I don't. Please, bring back my wood. I bought it fair and square and left it here, right in this spot."

She tilts her head. "Kirk told me I could use whatever I wanted. He said it's a neighborly place."

I stifle a groan and realize her world and mine are light years apart, and we'll never see eye to eye, no matter how much I try to straighten her out. "Kirk isn't king. You might consider how you'd feel if it was your wood and someone took it."

She giggles, putting her hand over her mouth. "I'd say have at it. Share and share alike. Nothing belongs to any one person, anyway."

I snort and shake my head. I've had enough nonsense tonight, so I come right out and say my truth. "That's a bunch of baloney, and I call it stealing."

She waves a hand, like it's no big deal. "Whatever."

Coming around the garage corner and striding up to

us, Dusty stops and shoves his hands in his jean pockets. He flashes a shy smile at Zoila. "Nice to hear laughter on a holiday. Where's the party? I'm in."

I purse my lips and swallow a snarky remark. These two deserve each other. At a glance, they both seem like me, my, mine, kind of people who take, take, take with little concern for others.

She laughs and plays with her hair, and I step back. My feet are cold from standing on snow-covered ground, and my shoulders are sagging. My muscles ache, and I'd like a long, hot shower and a sound night's sleep, but I won't have any of that tonight, not while Dusty is under my roof.

She smiles, eyeing him up and down. He bends to look her in the eye and says, "I'm Dusty, and you are?"

"Zoila, and I'm your mom's new neighbor."

"Mind if I look at your place? Haven't been in there for a long time. We could use some firewood too, if you've got it to lend to us."

She tilts her head. "Lend? I'd never lend firewood to a neighbor. I'd give it to them. Isn't that right, Jacklyn?"

I release a heavy sigh. "Goodnight. I'm going inside. Dusty, bring the firewood, will you?"

He nods at me and sneaks a glance at Zoila. These two are as thick as thieves and they've only just met. Good grief.

"Sure, Mom, whatever you say."

Snow mixed with sleet stings my face, and I watch

them walk away together. A wave of longing for my departed husband washes over me, and I stand alone in the snow, tears trickling down my cheeks. A new day is hours away, and I have much to do as the clock ticks down to daybreak.

44

KELLY

An alarm shrieks, giving me a horrible headache. Snow flies past, and slivers of pain shoot through my feet from standing on freezing pavement. My palms throb from bashing a big rock against the reinforced window, and my fingers are bleeding. My grandfather frowns a few feet away. He's breathing hard and wheezing.

I hold the snow shovel up in the air, gripping it tight, and say in a shaking voice, "Stay away from me. Mom was right. You're not family. You're a monster."

His brown eyes narrow, and his hands clench. "You're a spoiled brat."

My heart races. A trickle of sweat drips down my arms. Every nerve in my body is on alert, and I raise the shovel higher, bracing for impact.

Granddad lunges for the snow shovel, but I bring the blade down on his back. He collapses on the ground, moaning. His scalp oozes blood. He fingers the wound and gets up, eyes blazing, reaching out and trying to grab the shovel.

I leap away, like I learned in dance class. "Get away from me."

He bends over with his hands on his knees, panting and eying me. "You're coming with me, right now. You'll do extra chores at the cabin as punishment for this."

I shake my head. "You don't have a cabin. You only have a bad temper. I don't want to be near you, and I don't want to live by a river. I don't want to have anything to do with you ever again. Leave me alone."

He opens his arms, coming toward me. "Come with me and don't make trouble."

I brace my legs and scream with all my might. With the alarm going off, someone's got to arrive on the scene and help me. I can only hold him off for so long.

A thin guy in a dark hoodie and jeans runs out the back door, looking around. His eyes are wide, his mouth is open, and he holds a broom like a weapon in his shaking hands. "I had headphones on. What happened?"

Holding the shovel, I say, "My granddad abducted me. He's threatening me."

Granddad smiles. "It's not like that, not at all. She's my granddaughter and she wanted to use your bathroom. That's why she was trying to get inside."

I glare at him and say to the guy in the hoodie, "Don't believe a word he says. He's lying. He just got out of prison for killing a man."

45

———

IRENA

I smack a hand to my forehead and pick up my phone, calling my ex-husband, Jack. The call goes to voice mail, so I hang up and call my best friend Abby, who recently married Jack. It's been an odd time all around with shifting sand bars in the sea of life. What happened to Kelly is breaking my heart.

Abby answers the phone right away. "I saw you called Jack. What's up?"

I roll my eyes because it's just plain weird for my ex and my best friend to be paired up and thick as thieves. Except I guess they were that way before, but kept it a secret from me. "Are you sitting down?"

"Okay, I am now."

"Kelly was taken by my dad earlier today, and we're trying to find her."

Abby says, "Oh, no. Taken when?"

"Maybe three-thirty. We're trying to piece it together. The FBI and Violet and her team are working on finding her."

She raises her voice. "Why did you wait this long to tell us? Kelly's been gone for hours, and you're just now calling to let us know? What were you thinking?"

My throat tightens with tears. "I'm sorry. I forgot to call."

"You forgot to call? I can't believe it."

"I've been trying to get her back."

She says, "Tell me everything you know and fast. We'll help however we can."

I go over the murky details and when I mention Karina and Bernard canvassing the neighborhood, she says, "All this time, and you didn't think to call her father?"

"Like I said, I'm sorry."

"Keep going."

I tell her about a possible incident at a convenience store off I-5, and she screams in my ear. "Why didn't you tell me this first? It's happening now and it could be Kelly?"

I nod. "Yeah, but I don't know where it is or if it's Kelly. Violet told me to stay home, in case Kelly returns."

My laptop dings with a message, and I open it, saying to Abby, "Hold on, someone with a police scanner says it's a convenience store outside the town of Lancer."

"I've never heard of the place, have you?"

I swallow hard. "No, but I'll drive there to see if it's Kelly and do what I can."

Abby says, "You can't leave, in case she makes it home and the kid at the store isn't her. But I can go. I'll bring Jack to your place, and the dog too, and leave them with you while I drive there. She's my goddaughter, after all."

I cock my head and wish I was the one running to the rescue, instead of her. "Can your car handle the snow? It's coming down hard, and the freeway looks bad."

"It'll be fine. Stay there, and we'll be over soon."

I sigh, resting a hand on my thigh, and groan. "I'm not used to being the one sitting around waiting. I'm the one who runs to the rescue."

"Maybe it's time you learned to live on the slow side of life. It's not so bad."

I snort. "Not likely to happen. I'll see you soon."

46

JACKLYN

Dusty walks off with Zoila, and I frown, rubbing my hands together for warmth. Fat snowflakes coming down are chased by the wind. A tall fir tree in the front yard groans and sways, branches burdened with a thick layer of snow. I take in the still, silent neighborhood and shake my head. The world is in a sorry state if you can't trust your neighbors, who steal from you. I'll have to keep an eye on my new next-door neighbor.

Pushing against the wind and stomping through snow, I step into the garage to take a look around. I shiver in the cold and can see my breath. My son took two screwdrivers from the workbench, where I arranged them in order of size, and left the rest in disarray. One dropped on the floor, and I bend over to pick it up.

At a sound of a door opening, I bite my lower lip and

look around. No one is there. Being in close proximity to my conniving son is making me paranoid. Next thing I know, I'll see Sasquatch lumbering down the street in a snow storm.

The wind moans, and a branch lands with a loud thud on the garage roof. I jerk and jump in the air, every nerve on edge. My eyes dart around, and I tell myself there is no enemy here. It's all in my imagination.

Letting out a little chuckle, I pick up a screwdriver, tuck it under my coat and head inside.

47

VIOLET

When I call Special Agent Frankie McNalley, she answers on the first ring. "McNalley." Road noise is in the background, and it sounds like she's driving.

I say, "It's Violet. Did you find out if Kelly's at the convenience store off I-5?"

"Not yet. We're on our way but won't get there for at least an hour."

Her partner Mark Brick says, "State troopers should arrive on the scene soon."

Frankie adds, "We're doing all we can."

My voice trembles when I say, "Please keep me updated."

"It might be a while. Tell Irena we'll be in touch if we find her daughter."

I hang up and stride to the bullpen. Flora and Mimi

are bent over laptops, tapping on keyboards and staring at computer screens. I clear my throat. "The FBI agents don't know yet if Kelly's at that store or if some other unfortunate girl is fighting with an older man."

We whoosh out breaths and return to work. This will be a long night.

48

KELLY

The store alarm shrieks, and a siren in the distance is coming closer. My cheeks are wet with tears, and my teeth are chattering. I just have to hold out a little longer. Help is on the way.

Granddad steps toward me, but I move over to the store guy in the hoodie, who frowns. "You both have to cool it. The cops should be here any minute."

I point at Granddad and burst into tears. "He kidnapped me, and he should be arrested. I want to go home."

Granddad smirks, shoving his hands in his pockets. "She's family, and she wanted to go for a ride. It's not my fault."

My hands clench. "You're lying. You locked the doors and wouldn't let me out."

Mr. Hoodie shifts his weight from side to side and looks at his truck.

My head throbs with a headache. I've got to get away from Granddad. I want to go home.

Sirens grow louder, giving me hope it won't be long until I'm rescued. I count the seconds and tighten my grip on the shovel, glaring at Granddad. Thinking of the whip I tucked into the waist of my pants, I swallow and hope this nightmare will be over soon.

I stifle a sob, missing Mom. When I get home, I'll do whatever Mom wants. I'll study hard. I'll be polite. I'll help around the house. I'll go out on her boat whenever she asks, and I won't complain.

Granddad says to me, "Come on, this is our last chance to get away." He reaches out to grab my arm, but I run to the other side of Mr. Hoodie.

"Don't come any closer."

He points a tattooed finger at me. "We've got to go."

I shake my head, and Mr. Hoodie goes over to check the broken window. Granddad lunges for me, but I step aside, spinning away, like I learned in dance class. Granddad falls flat on his stomach in the snow.

I grimace and pull out the whip, cracking the air. "Stay away from me."

He slowly rises to his knees and narrows his dark eyes. "You're trouble, like your mother was. You'll learn not to mess with me, missy."

A white Washington State Patrol squad car with

flashing lights comes around the corner and pulls to a stop, turning off the siren and lights. I coil the whip and tuck it in the waist of my pants. My teeth chatter, my feet throb, and my hands hurt. Needles of pain jab at my toes.

Two troopers climb out of the car and come over. Granddad tiptoes along the side of the building, looking about to bolt, but an officer who is about my dad's age, in his forties, says in a gruff voice, "Don't move. Stay right there."

Granddad gulps, and his Adam's apple bobs up and down. A sheen of sweat covers his forehead. He leans back against the cement-block building and wheezes, coughing to catch his breath.

He shoots me a shifty side glance, but I look away. I used to feel sorry for him but that disappeared many hours ago, when he forced me in the car. My throat closes tight with tears. I recently gained a grandfather, which I thought was great, but tonight I lost him and the fairytale family I created in my mind.

An older trooper pushes his cap back, revealing a receding hair line, and rests his hands on his hips. "What's the problem here?"

I jab a finger at Granddad. "My grandfather kidnapped me. He locked the car doors and wouldn't let me out. I want to go home to my mom."

Granddad plasters a wide smile across his face. "Don't mind her and what she says. She's just acting up, like teenagers do. You know how they are. This is a private matter between family members, and I apologize for airing our dirty laundry in public. We'll be on our way."

I turn to the troopers and rub my arms, shivering. "Will you please put me in your car? My feet are getting numb, and I'm really cold."

Mr. Hoodie says, "I came out, and they were arguing. She broke the window."

Granddad points at the back door. "I'll pay for the window, no problem. She's my granddaughter, and she's got a temper, like her mother. Women, you know?"

A younger trooper hitches up his belt. "We have a report of a kidnapping, and you two match the descriptions."

My body quivers with rage, and I say in a loud voice, "Please, protect me from him and let me go home."

The older trooper eyes me. "How'd you end up in the car with your grandfather?"

I swallow. "He threatened me with a knife and made me get in his car."

The younger trooper says, "We need to verify your names and addresses."

The troopers talk to Mr. Hoodie, and Granddad sidles up to me and whispers in my ear, giving off a stench of bad breath and stale beef jerky. "Listen, kid, it's now or never. Run to the car with me, or you're headed to jail."

I tilt my head. "I'm not the one going to jail. You are."

He rubs his whiskered chin. "You broke the window.

You told me you wanted to run away. You lured me into all this. I'm the victim."

My mouth drops open. He's twisting the truth, but I can't let him get away with it.

He waves to the troopers. "Hey, over here, we have something to tell you."

The troopers turn, and I shake my head. "He's making up stories. He kept me in his car and wouldn't let me out."

Granddad opens his hands. "She came up with the idea to run away. This whole trip was her idea."

My pulse races. "Don't believe him. He just got out of jail. He's lying."

The older trooper studies my grandfather and rocks back on his heels. "Is that true? Were you recently released from jail?"

Granddad rolls his eyes. "That's not the point here. I kept her safe when she wanted to run away. Instead of being on the streets, I took her with me. Being with her granddad is far better than her being alone and vulnerable, wouldn't you agree?"

The older officer says. "Your story could be plausible, but we've had a report of a kidnapping, and she matches the description of the missing girl." He turns to me. "What's your name?"

"Kelly Fishbone. And this is my grandfather, Leonard Pickle."

Granddad says, "We're having a vacation and quality

time together. Even if she isn't enjoying the ride as much as I'd hoped, isn't that right, darling?"

I clench my fists. "He's making it up. I never wanted to run away. It's a lie. You can call my mother, and she'll tell you the truth."

The younger trooper arches an eyebrow. "Where was your mother when you left your house with your grandfather? Why didn't she stop you from leaving with him?"

I release a slow breath. "She wasn't home."

The older trooper turns to my grandfather. "Why were you in prison?"

Granddad shrugs. "It's no big deal. I served time for something that wasn't my fault, and I'm keeping to the straight and narrow, like I always do."

The younger officer taps a finger to his belt buckle. "Did your parole officer give you permission to be in this area?"

Granddad half-smiles. "Of course. Otherwise, I wouldn't be here, would I?"

The troopers step to the side, talking in low voices.

I'm shivering, and my teeth won't stop chattering.

The older trooper says, "We need to verify your story. We'll be right back."

My jaw drops. In a tear-choked voice, I say, "He tried to take me across the border into Canada. This is kidnapping. I was taken by force, and he locked me in the car. He's a liar."

The trooper tugs on the brim of his hat. "Wait here. We have to check on a few things.

I shiver. "I want to wait in the car, where it's warm."

"Okay, you can get in the back seat."

I stumble to the State Patrol car, slipping in snow and climbing inside. Sitting in the back seat, my pulse pounds in my ears, and my feet throb. The troopers talk and use the radio. Will they believe a criminal or a teenage girl? I never should have sent that text to Granddad. I should've believed my mother about his terrible temper.

Mr. Hoodie leans in the window of the patrol car and says, "I'm going inside. Goodnight. Hope you work it out. I have to get some sleep before I open tomorrow."

He marches inside and disappears, coming back and putting a piece of cardboard over the gaping hole in the window, where the glass is gone.

Granddad shuffles toward the Patrol car, extending his catcher's mitt-sized hands, and bends over the partly-opened window. He coughs and says in a hoarse voice, "Kelly, I'm sorry if you misunderstood all this. Let's get out of here. The river calls."

My muscles tense, ready to fight him off if I must. I scream, "Go away. I'm not leaving with you."

DUSTY

I walk arm in arm with the next-door neighbor and let out a sigh of relief. Despite snow flying into my eyes and the wind bearing down on my back, I'm out of Mom's overcrowded house. Her friends obviously don't like me, and I need to get away for a bit.

Zoila glances at me. "Everything okay? You seem tense about something. But I don't know you well enough to say that, do I, since we only just met?"

I lean over and whisper in her ear as we approach the steps to her house. "Come on, we can stop pretending, don't you think?"

She flashes a wide smile and opens the door, letting me inside.

IRENA

A car stops out front, and I fling open the door, wind rushing past my face. My best friend Abby is coming up the snow-covered walkway with Jack, my ex-husband. We used to talk every day before he hit his head and went missing. Then he married Abby and now our contact is limited. He's hers, not mine, and it's fine with me.

Jack's hair is short, not worn in the horrible Mohawk he used to wear with a braid in back. That was a terrible look, but I never told him that to his face. He's using a cane and hobbling. Happy, the dog they adopted when our friend Buzz met an untimely death, romps in the snow and rolls on his back.

I say, "Sorry, I didn't clear the walkway. I've been worried about Kelly."

Abby helps him up the steps, and he stops at the

threshold, giving me a hard look. I gesture inside. "Come in and warm up."

Abby helps him sit on the sofa. Happy runs inside, shakes off and rolls on the rug by the empty fireplace. I say, "Would you like me to make a fire? Or get you a cup of tea or coffee?"

"No," Jack says in a serious tone of voice. "I'd like you sit down and tell me why you didn't think to tell me our daughter was taken."

Abby pats his shoulder and moves to the door. "I'm off. It's the town of Lancer, right? I found it on the map but it's not much, just a store and farmland."

I jump up to hug her goodbye, but she steps back from my embrace and shakes her head. "You and I have some talking to do when this all settles down, which I hope it will, for Kelly's sake and for yours."

I cringe because she's never spoken this harshly to me, and we've been friends since high school. She turns and walks out, slamming the door behind her, and leaving me alone with my ex-husband.

I turn to Jack, who is glowering, and open my hands. "I've had a million things on my mind, so it's easy to understand how I forgot to contact you."

After a beat of silence, he says, "I'm disappointed in you."

My chest tightens, and I bend to pet the dog, rubbing his belly and distracting myself from the hard truth that I messed up. I look Jack in the eye. "I'm sorry. That's all I can say. Can we talk about what's happening?"

"Not yet. I want you to promise this will never happen again."

I nod and notice the spot where nurses shaved his head is growing in with downy hair. "Yes, I promise this will never happen again, because when Kelly comes home, she'll never leave my sight. If she stumbles and skins her knees in dance class from now on, I'll call you. I'll bother you about all the things, little and big."

He takes a cushion and holds it in front of him. "Good."

I draw a deep breath and ask what I've been waiting to, ever since he was released from the hospital. "Speaking of promises, how about you paying me back for the ten years of missing child support, starting next week?"

He looks down. "I'm getting my feet under me, and I can't pay you now, but I will as soon as I can."

I break down and weep, and he clumsily pats my back. When I'm cried out, I wipe my eyes and gaze at him. "We were good together, weren't we? When we were young? And when we were first married?"

His brown eyes fill with tears, and he looks at the dog. His grip tightens on the couch cushion. "I don't remember. I wish I could, but the past is gone, except for Abby and what happened on the wharf that night."

I sit back, stunned. For Jack to forget our past is like

the Salish Sea draining down to a muddy mess. Swallowing tears, I say, "Let's talk about Kelly."

51

GRANDDAD

After Kelly screams at me, I lean against the cement-block wall, trying to catch my breath. I was searching for family and to rebuild broken relationships, but my daughter wasn't interested. She made it impossible. And then, wonder of wonders, my granddaughter texted me.

My chest aches, and my left arm tingles. I wince as the pain moves to my jaw. My stomach sours, and I bend over, puking on the snow. I shuffle away from the stench, my mouth tasting of bitter bile.

I glance in Kelly's direction and shake my head. She didn't want to leave the house when I told her about my big adventure, and I lost my temper, forcing her into the car. Kids, what a pain in the butt.

My left arm goes numb. Slumping down on the cold ground, I whisper for help, but no one hears. A wash of fatigue sweeps over me, and I close my eyes. I'm alone, like I've always felt, even when surrounded by hundreds of people in prison. If this is how my time on earth ends, it'll be fine, fading away on a cold night.

I wheeze and cough on the cold hard ground. My pants are damp, and I'm not sure if it's from melted snow, or if I wet myself. My chest hurts, my arm is numb and my jaw aches. This was supposed to be the trip of a lifetime with my granddaughter, but instead I'm incapacitated in the middle of nowhere.

"Help," I say in a weak, wavering voice.

But no one hears me.

Snowflakes fly past, carried by a stiff breeze.

I close my eyes and whisper, "I'm sorry."

52

JACKLYN

I glance at the kitchen clock and say to Mary, who is pouring coffee, "Dusty has been gone a long time. Wonder what's taking him so long."

Mary snickers. "Do I have to spell it out for you? She's an attractive woman and he's a handsome man."

I wince and hold up my hands. "Stop right there. Don't say anything more."

She smiles. "Don't be such a prude. Get with the times."

I shake my head. Serving coffee and after dinner drinks, I overhear Rose chatting with Bernice about buying a house. I wish I could help her, but my son siphoned off my funds. I won't sleep soundly when we're tucked in tonight, if he returns. I'll keep one eye open for his next attempt to submarine my independence.

53

FRANKIE

I drive down I-5, heading south from Seattle as fast as is safely possible, which means we're at a slow crawl in the fast lane with piles of snow along the side of the road. Only two lanes on the freeway are open. Cars have been abandoned in the snow in the right lane and on the far-right shoulder.

I frown. "We've got to get there to see if it's Kelly. How far is it to that town?"

Brick glances at his phone. "Forty-five minutes in good weather. The way this is going, it could take two or three hours."

I clench my jaw, flicking on the siren and flashing lights. "We don't have that luxury tonight. It's our job to protect a missing child of tender years."

Cars slowly move out of the way, but not fast enough for my liking.

Brick glances over. "Tender years is generally defined as a child twelve years or younger for kidnapping investigations, but I think we're making the right call by looking into this case."

I swallow and my throat is dry as I maneuver around stranded cars. "Definitely. Her grandfather tried to take her into Canada. That counts."

Brick points at a man in a business suit waving, with the hood of his car raised. "Wish we could stop and help him, but we can't. We've got to keep going."

I grip the steering wheel tight and stare ahead. The tires whine, and finally, the road opens up. "I agree. Why don't you call the State Patrol and ask if State troopers have arrived at the scene."

He pulls out his phone. "Roger that."

54

IRENA

Jack's jaw drops, and he massages his temples. "Your dad came to town and took Kelly?"

I let out a sigh. "He's mean and has a temper. I didn't want Kelly anywhere near him. His way of solving arguments is to beat people to a pulp."

Jack cringes. "I never met him, did I?"

"No, you didn't. He was sent to prison when I was young, and my mom put me in the car, driving west to get away from him. She didn't want him to find us. Mom was hurt by him, and his nickname wasn't Rattlesnake for nothing. But he went too far a bar fight in Eastern Washington, and a man died. That's how my dad ended up in prison."

I swallow tears for our daughter and twist my hands. "I'm sorry I didn't protect her better. This is all my fault."

He reaches over and pats my knee. "I've made my own

share of mistakes. It should be me asking you to forgive me. I should've paid you child support, I should've gotten a job and held on to it. I should've been a better man."

I wrap my arms around him, and we sob for the loss of our daughter and the mistakes we've made. After a minute, I pull away and wipe my eyes. "Let's start over again, and let go of what was in the past."

He shrugs. "I don't remember it anyway, so it's easy for me to let it go."

I blow my nose on a tissue and stand. "The slate is clear, except for the money you owe me. Now let's call the FBI agents and find out what's going on."

55

FRANKIE

Brick calls the State Patrol to ask about the incident at a convenience store off I-5 in Lancer, where a girl is screaming about her grandfather abducting her. He listens for a few moments and says, "Please patch me into an officer at the scene. I'd like to speak with them."

He drums his fingers on the seat and waits until someone comes on the line. Nodding, he says, "Because of the car make, model and license plate, we believe this is a case of an estranged grandfather trying to take a minor across state lines. He tried to cross into Canada, but they were turned back from the border."

A man says something, and Brick frowns. "Hold on, I'll put you on speaker phone. My partner Special Agent Frankie McNalley is here with me. Will you repeat what you just said?"

"Sure, I said we don't believe this is a case of kidnapping or abduction. We just spoke with the grandfather, who said this was the girl's idea. She wanted to run away from home, and instead of letting her do that, he took her on a trip, to keep her safe, so she wouldn't be out on the streets."

Another trooper chimes in. "Besides, where was the mother in all this? She wasn't even around. You'd think she'd have stayed home on a holiday with her daughter. What happened is her doing. If there's blame to sling around, it doesn't rest with the granddad, but on the mother's shoulders."

I roll my eyes. Everyone's an expert in parenting, it seems, and family matters, until it comes to their own household. Clearing my throat, I say, "We don't need to blame the mother right now. We need to keep the kid safe. Let's back up a few steps. Did you check their ID's? Run their names through the database?"

"Sure did," says the first trooper. "The grandfather was up front about having just got out of prison, and he said he had permission from his parole officer to be in the area."

I shake my head and keep driving on I-5 in the dark. Wiper blades swish back and forth, sweeping snowflakes from the windshield. We're one of a handful of cars moving south.

Brick leans forward in his seat and says in a clear, calm voice, "He's lying. We spoke with his parole officer, and he missed his last check in. He's not supposed to be in Western Washington. We have a statement from a neighbor across from the girl's home who said it looked like he marched the girl down the front steps and made her get in the car. As I said, he tried to take her into Canada, but they were turned back at the border. We don't believe this is a fun family trip, but an abduction of a young teenage girl."

"Sounds like we'd better re-think this then."

Brick nods. "What did the girl say?"

The second trooper says, "The girl?"

I say, "Yes, what did the girl say about what was happening? Did you get her statement? Where is she right now? In your car?"

The first trooper says in a deep voice, "She accused her grandfather of kidnapping her, but we thought it was a teenage tantrum, like he said. We've all seen how difficult kids can be, haven't we?"

Brick and I exchange a quick glance. Brick says into the phone, "Where is Kelly? Have you got her somewhere safe? We should be there in under twenty minutes."

"She was in the back seat, but she just ran out towards her grandfather."

I bark out, "Get her somewhere safe. Keep her away from him."

A girl screams in the background on the other end of the line, and hairs on my arms stand on end.

"We have a situation," the first trooper says, "got to go."

He hangs up, and Brick turns to me. "I hope we can rely on them to keep Kelly safe until we get there."

I shudder and drive through the snowy night. My muscles tense, ready to pull Kelly away from harm.

56

DUSTY

At my mom's next-door neighbor's place, I sprawl out on the sofa with my boots off and wait for Zoila to bring me a drink. She calls from the kitchen, "Two fingers of booze or three?"

I chuckle. "This has been one wild day and it isn't over yet. Better make it three. And only two ice cubes, no more."

She comes out and hands the drink to me. "Okay, partner in crime, what's the situation report? Have you found her checkbook yet?"

My stomach sours, and I sit up, making room for her, and shake my head. "Nope, not yet. But I think she's hidden something valuable in a ceiling vent in her study. I need to sneak in there while everyone's sleeping tonight."

She pouts, full red lips pushing out. "Spend the night here."

I toss back a slug of whiskey and grimace as I swallow. "What's this? Kerosene?"

She shrugs. "Some of us can't afford the best. That's why I signed on with you."

I set my glass on the rug. "Buy something better if you want me to come around. I'm a single malt kind of guy."

She sips wine and eyes me over the rim of the glass. "How much is your mother worth?"

I stand and shove my hands in my jeans pockets. "I'm not telling you that. Your job is to watch her and report any suspicious activities."

She screws up her face. "You mean like the older guy with the long beard coming around? He strikes me as odd."

"Not him. He's harmless, as long as my mom doesn't include him in her will."

She crosses her long legs. "What then? Give me a few more examples of what you're looking for."

"How late is she staying up? I need to know that so I can sneak in and reclaim a few things she neglected to give me. Does she have any other new friends I should know about? Did she drive home with a brand-new car or show other signs of spending her money in a flashy way?"

She puts down her glass and gets up, pulling her blue velvet robe tight around her waist. "What's this all about, really? Bottom line is it isn't normal to spy on your mother."

I rub my right cheek and grin. "Let's just say she owes

me for taking away my company, and I'm concerned for her financial welfare."

She rolls her eyes. "Sounds fishy to me, but I'll do it. I need the cash. I'll take your first payment now, in fact." She opens her hand and looks up at me, waiting.

"That's not how this works. I'm in charge and I'll tell you when you'll get paid. You haven't given me enough valuable information to make it worth my while."

She frowns and holds out her hand. "That's not how I do things. Pay up."

I scowl and turn away, scooping up an armload of firewood. "Hold the door for me, will you?"

She purses her lips, crossing her arms. "Why should I help you for no money? There's nothing in it for me."

I stagger with the firewood in my arms to the door. "It'll be worth it later on down the road."

She shakes her head. "No way. I'm a pay up front kind of gal. You promised me a Benjamin."

"Well, circumstances changed, and I'm dead broke."

I attempt to open the front door, and firewood tumbles out of my hands, wood chips and split logs flying in the air. I blow out a breath and put my hands on my hips, considering what to do. I want her to watch Mom and report in from next door. "Listen, how about we split the profit of whatever I find? Eighty percent for me, twenty for you."

She stares at the ceiling. "I'll take fifty-fifty, or it's no deal."

I bend and stack firewood, mulling over her offer. I'll take more than my share, but she'll never suspect it. To sound like I'm protesting, I let out a groan and say, "Fine."

I stand, arms full of wood, and she opens the door for me. "Don't come back for more. I need some too, you know."

I bite back a remark about her stealing from my mother and stride outside, carrying firewood in my arms. Snowflakes fly into my eyes, blinding me, and I slip on a step, tumbling down to a walkway. I land with a thud on my backside with wood scattered all around. With a grunt, I get up, rubbing my tailbone and stacking the wood.

I head next door, being careful where I step, and nod to myself. Everything has been going against me since Mom came home from Shore Lodge, but tonight I'll turn it around. I'll sneak in the study and find whatever she hid in the ceiling vent. If I'm lucky, it'll make me a very rich man. It could be cash or Treasury bonds or gold bars. All I know is when she protects a truth and hides something, it's generally worth my while to uncover it and find a way to take advantage of her.

Struggling through snow with my arms full, I approach her bungalow's front door and come up with a quick plan. I'll be nice and ingratiate myself, so that way she won't suspect I'm working behind her back. If it comes down to it, maybe Mom needs to have a fatal accident.

57

KELLY

I run back to the State Patrol car and yank on the back door handle, but it's locked. Pounding on the window, I yell. My hands are bruised, my legs are trembling, and even though I hate my grandfather, he needs help.

The younger trooper hops out, opens the back door and gestures inside. "Go ahead, get in while we sort this out."

I slide into the seat and burst into tears. "He's having a heart attack. I think he's dying." I point at my grandfather, sprawled on the pavement by the building.

The younger trooper says, "I'll go check."

I cross my arms and shiver, watching him hurry through snow to my grandfather. Tears stream down my cheeks. Wiper blades moan, slapping back and forth.

The trooper's voice comes over the radio. "We need an ambulance. Looks like he might've had a heart attack."

58

ABBY

Driving down the freeway, I grip the wheel tight and listen to the news, which is enough to make anyone feel tense. I turn off the radio and sing to myself but give it up after a few minutes. This isn't a night for rejoicing or song. It's time to recover my new husband's daughter from harm.

The car ahead skids, turning around and facing me head on.

I step on the brakes, but don't even begin to slow down, skidding on the slick pavement. Everything seems to move in slow motion as my car plows ahead toward disaster.

I scream, but the car barrels ahead. Metal crunches into metal, before everything goes black.

59

KELLY

Hunched over in the back of the patrol car, tears trickle down my cheeks while I wait for an ambulance to arrive. I don't want Granddad to die. If he passes away, I'll have to live with that memory for the rest of my life.

"Stay here," the older trooper says, climbing out of the car. He shakes a finger at me. "Don't move until I come back."

He slams the door, and I'm left alone. I hate the man that he is, but I don't wish him dead. I drop my grandfather's whip on the floor of the squad car and wince at how he suddenly lashed out, using the weapon. Releasing a breath, I realize how close I came to being hidden away with an angry, vengeful man for the rest of my life. I wish I could call my mom. She must be frantic with worry.

Sirens draw closer and an ambulance pulls up, cutting

the ear-splitting sound and flashing lights. Two people hop out and hurry to Granddad, bending over him and giving me second thoughts about staying in the car.

I pull on the backseat door latch and try to open it, but it won't budge. I yell and wave my hands to the younger trooper, who is standing away from the action, closer to the car. He turns, and I cup my hands, calling, "Let me out."

He nods and strides over, opening the car door, and I run to my grandfather's side. EMTs load him on a stretcher and wheel him toward the ambulance.

My throat is tight with tears. "Goodbye, Granddad."

His mouth goes slack, and his head flops to the side.

"Stand back," an EMT says in a harsh voice.

I step away and my mouth hangs open as the ambulance pulls away. What have I done? I've single-handedly wrecked the world my mom carefully constructed by sending a text that led to me being taken and trapped. I bite my lip and shake my head at how close I came to being hidden in a cabin, where no one would find me.

I stumble over to the State Patrol car, tumble inside and slump down on the seat, weeping for the havoc I caused.

A dark SUV pulls into the lot, and two FBI agents who helped my father jump out and run over to me. I burst into fresh tears. I'm safe. I'm one of the lucky ones who gets to go home.

60

JACKLYN

Someone thumps on the door, and I rush over. "It must be Dusty with the firewood." I fling it open, and he staggers in, dropping a load of wood by the fireplace. He wipes a bead of sweat from his brow and smiles, opening his arms and giving me a hug.

Patting his broad back, my eyebrows arch at his unexpected gesture of affection. My shoulders drop down and a flicker of hope rises up within me. I whisper, "I love you."

"Love you too," he says in a low voice. He steps back, but a flicker of angst flashes across his face before he clears his throat and says, "Everyone okay in here? Anyone need anything?"

Bernice chuckles from her spot on the rug, leaning against the wall. "Thanks, we're set. You mom is treating us well, as always."

Del from Shore Lodge says, "It's been a long day for me. If it's all right, I'll hit the hay. I can curl up in a corner if you tell me where to go. I know you don't have beds for us all."

Mercury and I exchange a glance, and he adjusts the red polka dot bow tie clipped to his long gray beard. He's not afraid to be different, and we're cut from the same cloth, since I give very few figs about what others say.

Mercury stands. "Sorry, we didn't make it to my place, Del. I'll find you a spot and get you a blanket."

Del yawns, covering his mouth. "Thanks, I'll be fine anywhere."

Dusty bends over the fireplace, crumpling newspaper and stacking kindling. "Most of us can sleep out here."

At a heavy thud outside the house, we gasp, and I flinch. Lights in the living room flicker and blink off. The house is dark. The refrigerator quits its dull humming and goes quiet. Clapping a hand to my chest, I hurry to the window and stare at a tall fir tree down across my front yard.

"At least we have heat," I say, walking to the hall closet and opening the door. But the furnace shuts off, suddenly silent.

I whoosh out a breath. "Sorry to say this, but the power is out, the heat's off, and we're snowed in. I'll light candles and gather flashlights. Dusty will get a fire going. We'll get through this and be the closer for it, don't you think?"

He says, "I'm not sure how long this wood will last. The neighbor refused to give us more and said she needs it for her place."

I frown and fumble in the dark, locating a flashlight in the dining room that I keep on hand for power outages. I'll deal with my new neighbor later. Right now I have bigger concerns on my mind, with a houseful of dinner guests.

Worry sprouts like a fast-growing weed, as I find more flashlights in a kitchen drawer and hand them out to those in the living room. I click on my flashlight and put it up at my chin in what might look like a ghoulish joke and say, "Well, we're trapped together tonight without power and heat. This will be a long night, but dawn will break, as it does every day. We'll make it to morning, when the sun will shine, and the town's solo snow plow will arrive at some point. So, we'll hunker down and hold out until then and, I hope, have a jolly holiday."

"Well said," Mary says. "And goodnight."

"Night," Del says from a dark corner.

Bernice and her friend chime in. "Goodnight."

"Sleep tight," Rose says, taking Max into the spare bedroom and closing the door.

The others may rest, but I still have much to do.

61

FRANKIE

Brick and I stride over to the State Patrol troopers, and I say, "Is Kelly in there?"

An older trooper nods. "Yep, we've got her safe and warm."

Brick looks around. "Where's her grandfather?"

"He might've had a heart attack," a younger trooper says. "The EMT's just left with him."

I frown. "Did you tell the EMTs that he's a convicted felon?"

The troopers shrug. "With all that was going on, it got swept under the rug."

I blow out a breath and think fast. "We can take the girl, but will you go to the hospital and make sure her grandfather is handcuffed to the bed? He'll likely try to escape, being as how this'll send him back to prison."

The older trooper touches his cap. "Well, that's if he

makes it. Some of them re-offend to get sent back, where they have three meals a day and don't have to work."

"Just make sure you keep him in handcuffs until one of our agents picks him up."

He nods. "You bet."

I turn to Brick, "Let's go get our girl."

The younger trooper taps on his belt buckle. "You know her?"

Brick says, "Her father went undercover for us, and we met her then. The Pacific Northwest isn't so big, especially north of Seattle."

We hurry through snow to the State Patrol cruiser and pull open the door. Kelly tumbles out of the car and into my arms, sobbing. I sling an arm around her trembling shoulders. "Come on, kid, let's take you home. Your granddad is headed back to prison for kidnapping."

We walk to my car, and I hand her a blanket before I hop in the driver's seat. Brick helps Kelly get in and sits beside her, helping her buckle up. She shudders and pulls the blanket tight around her. "The State Troopers believed Granddad, not me. He lied and said this whole trip was my idea."

Looking in the rear-view mirror, I lock eyes with Brick. This poor girl. "Your grandfather must spin a good tale, but it doesn't mean he won't come to justice. We'll get him for what he did."

"Good." Kelly sighs and slumps against Brick's shoulder as I drive away, turning up the heat for Kelly so she can thaw out. She falls fast asleep by the time I merge onto I-5 heading north, and I say to Brick, "Can you believe it? She was barefoot and freezing cold in the snow."

"How traumatizing."

I glance in the rear-view mirror and see a glint in Kelly's eyes, but she quickly closes them. Snow is falling, and few cars are out just before midnight. The road is fairly clear in the fast lane, and I have snow tires, so I push on the accelerator and lean forward, willing us north to Kelly's mom's open arms.

I'm lost in my thoughts when Brick says, "We'd better let Irena know we have her. I'll do it since you're driving."

A car to my right starts to enter my lane, and I lay on the horn, honking.

Kelly opens her eyes, looking around in a panic. "What was that? Is he here, coming for me?"

"You're safe now, and he's at a hospital. He won't be coming after you again."

"Good. I want to call my mom. Can I use your phone?"

Brick pulls out his cell. "I'll dial, and we'll put it on speaker."

"Okay."

A moment later, Irena answers. "Hello?"

"Mom, it's me. I'm safe. I'm coming home."

"Oh, my love. I was going out of my mind and frantic worrying about you. This is all my fault."

Kelly shakes her head. "No, it's my fault. I'm sorry I

didn't listen to you. The FBI agents are bringing me home." She says to Brick, "I mean, aren't you? Or do I have to go in and give a statement or something?"

"You're not a suspect," I say. "We'll take you home and get your statement there."

"Mom, I'll see you soon. I love you."

"Love you too, Kels, with all my heart."

62

DUSTY

Mom hands out flashlights and gives a little uplifting speech, but it falls flat. The mood in the living room is as dark as the house. I run through a ream of possible ideas for how to take advantage of the situation and say, "Mom, why don't you check with the neighbors? Maybe their power isn't out and some of us can go spend the night there and stay warm."

"That's a very good idea," she says. "I'll call Bernard Frackus right now. I hope I won't wake him up, but it would be great if he has heat."

Del says, "If we have to split up, I'll go to a neighbor's place."

Mom pulls out her phone. "Hold on, we'll see what he says."

I stand close to her to listen in.

Bernard picks up on the first ring. "Jacklyn? Why're you calling this late?"

"I didn't know if you're up and you noticed, but a tree fell on a power line, and we don't have lights or heat over at my house. Do you have power?"

He says in a tense voice, "I'm not home, haven't been home for hours. Have you heard the news?"

I shake my head, overhearing their conversation. Mom is speaking at half-speed compared to him. Pick up the pace, I want to tell her, but I bite back the words. I've got to stay on her good side for as long as I can, so she'll trust me and won't watch while I wander around her house.

Tapping a finger to my lips, I make a plan. I'll comb through her purse, check her pockets while she's asleep, unscrew the ceiling vent and search her freezer to see if she hid anything important there. When I was growing up, she'd hide stuff and forget where it was stashed. Dad and I would hunt for the missing item and make it into a game, so I have a pretty good idea of where she might hide emergency cash and valuables. Of course, since I emptied out her place, she may have picked up some new habits.

Bernard's voice cuts through my thoughts. "Kelly's been taken."

"Whoa," I say, letting out a low whistle.

Mom says in a loud voice, "When? How? What can I do to help?"

"No need to get alarmed. She's been found."

I release a sigh and clap Mom on the back.

She leans into me, like she used to before Dad died, and says to Bernard, "Oh my gracious. What a shock to the system. Talk about a fruit basket upset."

Bernard chuckles. "I'm not sure what you mean by that, but yes, it's been very upsetting. Karina and I are over at Violet's office. We've been helping where we can, trying to track her down."

The rest of the group gathered in the living room is abuzz with the news, talking in low, urgent voices. Candles flicker as Del walks up to us. "Can some of us sleep there?"

Mom repeats the request, and Bernard says in the stern, matter of fact tone that I remember from when he was my high school science teacher, "Sorry to say the house is locked up tight, and with this weather, we're stuck in place. I won't be able to get home tonight and maybe not tomorrow, depending on when the town's only snow plow gets going."

Mom's jaw drops. "You mean the snow plow isn't out, clearing the roads?"

"No, it's Christmas Eve, and I heard they had trouble tracking the driver down."

I say, "Do you have a spare key we could use to get in your place?"

"No hide-a-key for me. It wouldn't be safe, you know. Hope you can stay warm."

We say goodbye, and Mom hangs up. "At least we tried."

Mary says, "What about your other neighbors?"

Mom shrugs. "The rest are away for the holidays. We're stuck with our situation."

Del tugs his earlobe. "What about the woman next door? Let's ask her."

I shake my head. "I'd avoid her place. She plays drums all night."

I open the door, and the crashing of snare drums drifts across the lawn.

Mom says, "You've made your point, Dusty. Close the door."

63

———

JACKLYN

Dusty closes the door, and I glance at my son, wondering how he knows my next-door neighbor so well. Are they in cahoots with each other? Rose comes over to us and says in a low voice, "It's almost midnight. Will we do our toast, like when Dad was alive?"

I rest a hand on my heart and remember my big-hearted husband. Patting my grown children's shoulders, I say, "I guess we should carry on with family traditions in his absence. Your father would want us to."

Bernice pipes up. "Let's sit by the fire while we have the toast. It's nice and warm here."

Mercury sidles up to me. "What can I do to help you?"

Dusty steps between us, which is rude. I've gotten to know my son's true self since his dad died, and I know the dark depths lurking below his surface demeanor.

Crossing my arms, I wonder how this night will end. He's the same sneaky son who took my money. But this time, instead of Cedar Channel separating us, he's right under my roof and will stay here until the snow plow comes through.

I wince and reflect that although I don't trust Dusty, or his new façade of pretending to be kind, I'm holding out hope that he'll grow and change for the better. I release a sigh, because a thorny blackberry bush remains the same, no matter how much you want it to become a daisy.

Dusty smiles at me. "I'll get the party hats. Dad would want me to do that."

I purse my lips and nod. "Fine."

He strides away, and Buddy trots after him, perhaps wanting a treat. I exchange a quick look with Mercury, roll my eyes and whisper in his ear. "I don't know how we're going to get through tonight with the power out and everyone here."

He pecks me on the cheek. "We're in it together. I'll help hold down the fort."

"Thanks, I could use the assist."

Soon, we're gathered in the living room, some sitting on the floor with me, others on the sofa or in camp chairs. Dusty takes the one nice upholstered arm chair. Elastic from the party hat tugs at my chin. Looking around the group, a lump forms in my throat, and I raise a glass of champagne. "This is a special evening, and I'm glad to see you here. To many more Christmas Eve's together!"

Mary throws me an air kiss and sips from her glass.

"Cheers to that," Fred says from the floor, firelight flickering across his face.

Letting out a sigh, I say, "We'll all feel better when the snow plow comes through, tomorrow, I hope."

Rose groans. "We might be stuck for days."

Dusty pulls at elastic under his chin. "They cover downtown before residential areas. We're down the list in terms of their priorities, and it might take a while."

Bernice sips her drink and smiles. "Remember that big storm that blew through in March a few years ago? I was socked because of the snow for two days before they came down our street."

Del frowns. "Does this town really only have one snowplow? That's nuts."

Fred shrugs. "There's not much need for it some years, so they get by with what they have."

I lean against the wall, sipping chilled, bubbly champagne, and hope the stack of wood Dusty brought in will last until morning. My son stares at me with flat brown eyes, and a shiver runs up my spine. I'm not looking forward to a long night of sharing space with him, not at all.

64

DUSTY

I help Mom hand out blankets and get everyone settled for the night in my new role of adoring, supportive son. Despite the dim candlelight, I see a frown flicker across her face when she sees me coming toward her. When I was growing up, she'd suddenly appear, ready to pounce on my mischievous misdeeds. One time I was drawing on the neighbor's fence with charcoal, and she came out yelling, making me scrub my artwork off with a sponge and soapy water.

Now I glance around the living room and say in a soft voice, "I think that's it."

She whispers, "It's as good as it's going to get, considering the circumstances."

Del snores from a corner of the living room. Bernice and her friend whisper in the dark. Mary and Fred are on the sofa, crammed side by side close together.

A gust of wind hits the house, and a roof shingle skitters and falls, landing on the window sill with a thud. I glance out at the front yard, buried in fresh snow, and whisper to Mom, who is standing by my side looking out. "Must be two feet of snow."

"Yes, it's pretty, isn't it?"

"Measuring is pretty important when you run a construction business."

She rubs her arms. "I get that. I'm excited about learning on the job."

I bite back a bitter remark, wanting to say how expensive that will be and how some vendors will take advantage of her innocence. Instead, I clear my throat. "Would you like to wear my coat to stay warm?"

She touches my elbow. "Thanks, but I'm fine, at least for now."

I head to the kitchen for a glass of water, and she joins me. I turn off my phone's flashlight and we stand at the kitchen sink staring out the window at the changed landscape. The lawn, her garden and evergreen trees are covered with snow that almost glows in the dark. I fill a glass with tap water, gulp it down and hope she won't follow me around all night, because I have plans for when the others are asleep.

She turns to me. "Where are you sleeping?"

I shrug. "I thought I'd crash in your study, since everywhere else is full."

She shakes her head. "That room is off limits. No one's going in there."

I open my hands. "Come on, it's an empty room. We might as well use it."

She puts her hands on her hips. "Go in your old bedroom."

I wrinkle my nose. "And camp out with Rose and Max? Come on. That room is tiny. There's no space on the floor for me. I won't even fit in the closet. But maybe we can move Max into the closet, now that you mention it."

She taps a finger to her chin. "I see your point. Tell you what, I'll let you in, but don't touch my things." She gives me a steely-eyed glance and points a finger at my chest.

I flinch from her intensity and hold up my hands, stepping back from her know-it-all jabbing finger. "Hey, don't worry about it. When will you learn to trust me and let bygones be bygones?"

She scowls by the window and suddenly her face looks lined and old. "I don't think I'll ever forgive and forget what happened at Shore Lodge. I don't appreciate your making light of it."

We stand gripping the cool porcelain sink in dead silence for a moment. I stay utterly still and barely breathe to have a better chance of winning the battle. All I need is twenty minutes alone in the study to improve my chances of being a rich man.

I rest a hand on my heart, missing my father, because I

know Dad would want me to take more of her money. He laughed when I jokingly referred to his large gifts to me as my early inheritance. Dad would straighten up in his reading chair in the living room and put a finger to his lips, saying, "Don't mention this to your mother. She can't ever know." But after he passed away, Mom combed through their financial records and discovered what he'd done. She cut off my financial lifeline, and I'm still oozing with resentment over her hard-hearted cruel act. A mother should support her son.

Mom whispers, "Follow me."

She flicks on her flashlight and goes down the dark hall, stopping at the study. She pulls out a key, unlocks the door and swings it open. The door creaks.

I pat her shoulder, and she stiffens. I say in a soft voice, "I'll oil the hinges in the morning. Night, Mom."

She nods and moves toward her bedroom door. "Sleep well, son. Tomorrow is a brand-new day."

I tiptoe into the study, grasp the cool metal door knob and gently close the door. The room is quiet. With the power out, all the electronics are off. The air is stuffy, as if the room hasn't been used much since Dad died.

I turn on my phone's flashlight app and scan the room. My gaze lands on my father's side of the room. I set my phone down on his desk and sit in Dad's office chair, spinning around and lifting my legs like a little kid. I whisper, "I miss you, Dad. You'll never know how much."

65

JACKLYN

My dog pads down the hall, joining me in my bedroom. I leave the door ajar in case anyone wakes up and needs something. I climb into bed with my clothes and wool knit hat on for warmth. Staring at the ceiling, I blink at how I'm hosting the strangest surprise sleepover with others stranded in a storm.

I grab my phone, look up the power company online and send a text message saying my power is out. Buddy curls up in his dog bed on the floor and lets out a deep sigh.

I turn in the dog's direction and say in a soft voice, "Good night, sweet pup. See you in the morning."

I close my eyes but sleep doesn't come, because I'm sure that right across the hall, my son is trying to undo my financial independence and take what he believes he deserves. I whisper to Buddy, "But he has no idea who he's up against, does he?"

66

IRENA

A dark SUV pulls up to the curb and parks, and I fly out of the house, slipping on the front walkway that I shoveled while anxiously waiting for my daughter's return. Special Agent Mark Brick climbs out and holds the door open for Kelly. She crashes into my open arms, sobbing, and I wrap my arms around her, holding on tight. I say, "I've never been so frightened."

Special Agent Frankie McNalley comes around the car. "Let's get her inside. She's been through a lot."

I slide an arm around Kelly's shoulder, guiding her inside. "Come on, I'll make hot cocoa, and you can tell me what happened."

Kelly stumbles to the front door, and I support her weight. My darling light-hearted daughter left and has been replaced by a shipwreck.

I glance down at her feet. "Where are your shoes?"

She blinks and wipes tears from her wet cheeks. "Granddad told me to get in the car. We left the house in a hurry, and I lost my slippers in the snow when I ran away from him."

We burst through the doorway and collapse on the couch, and I bite my lip. Tears stream down my face, but I gather my wits and tell myself to get it together. Kelly needs a mother to tend to her needs.

"Hold on," I say, "I'll be right back."

I get up and grab some rubbing alcohol wipes and soft thick socks. "I'm sorry but this might hurt." She winces when I clean cuts on her feet and gently pull socks over her swollen toes. "Rest here, and let's put your feet up."

She lets me swing her feet up onto the couch. Her teeth chatter non-stop, and she's shivering. I tuck blankets over her and add a nylon sleeping bag over that, with a knit cap on her beautiful head. She hiccups and closes her eyes.

"There," I say, hands on my hips. "You look like a big burrito wrapped in foil."

She almost giggles. I take a deep breath, reminding myself to hold it together until I'm alone to let it out and cry. "I'll be right back with your hot chocolate."

She says in a weak voice, "With marshmallows?"

I kiss Kelly's damp cheek. "You can have anything you want."

Special Agent McNalley and Brick come in the room,

and I gesture to two arm chairs. "Make yourselves at home. I'll be in the kitchen getting her a hot drink."

McNalley nods to me. "I'd like to speak with you in private for a moment."

Brick sits and eyes Kelly. "You're safe now, Kelly."

She keeps her eyes closed, and her body shakes, but she releases a little sigh.

I say, "I'll be right back. I'll be in the kitchen, making you hot cocoa. I love you with all my heart."

In the kitchen, I heat milk for hot cocoa and rummage in a cupboard, pulling out a bag with marshmallows. McNalley leans on the counter. "Your daughter has been through a traumatic event, and she'll need support after this."

I nod and stir milk, spooning in cocoa powder and adding vanilla extract. "Tell me exactly what happened."

She frowns. "Your father wanted to take her into Canada on his way to Alaska. He was apparently planning on hiding out at a derelict fishing shack on a river someone told him about when he was in prison."

I gasp, because if he'd been successful, I might not have seen my daughter again. I blink back tears. "What else?"

"He wouldn't let her out of the car. He forced her at knife point to get in the car in the first place, and he drove south on I-5 after they were turned back from the border. We believe he was heading to the Columbia River, on the Washington State side."

As I stir, milk slops over the edge of the pan, sizzling on the hot burner. "What can I do to help her deal with this?"

"She'll need counseling. She may have nightmares. She'll need support from family."

I gulp, thinking of bills on my desk waiting to be paid. "You think I shouldn't work for a while?"

"I'd advise you take a week or two off to be with her around the clock. She's been through a traumatic event."

I wince and whisper, "He wouldn't let her out of the car?"

"No, and as you saw, her feet look pretty messed up from the ordeal. There may be long-term impacts from what she experienced, physically and emotionally."

I pour cocoa into a mug, adding five tiny marshmallows and taking a deep breath. "Thanks for filling me in," I say and hurry out to help my damaged daughter. I'll do anything I can to heal her and bring her back to health.

Entering the living room, I frown as a thought crosses my mind. I should have asked where my father is, but I won't do that in front of Kelly and disturb her. As long as he's alive, we'll never be safe.

67

IRENA

Kelly sits up and sips hot chocolate while the FBI agents ask questions about her ordeal, and she answers in a flat tone of voice. I sit beside her, rubbing circles on her back, like I did when she was little and had a skinned knee. Except this is much bigger. I clench my jaw and consider how my dad's cruel criminal act ripped away the young girl I knew and replaced her bright eyes and bubbly remarks with dull eyes and a somber expression.

My jaw drops when I hear how my dad tried to cross into Canada with her.

Kelly's lips tremble. "He went crazy when we had to turn around. I thought he was going to hit me."

My pulse quickens, and my chest tightens with fear. I'm thrown back to my childhood and how he lashed out at my mother. I grit my teeth and release a slow breath.

Kelly talks about how she fled from the car and ran for her life through deep snow. My stomach churns with acid, and I bend over, resting a hand on it. If my dad was here, I'd make him tremble with fear and wipe his smug smile off his face. I will not rest until he's back in prison for the rest of his life.

Kelly sets down her half-empty mug with a thud, and I blink. She always drinks all of her hot cocoa, because she loves it that much. She sighs and says, "I'm tired."

I touch her arm. "You rest, and I'll be right here, taking care of you."

I stand, and she curls up on the sofa. I pull the sleeping bag and blankets over her.

Agents McNalley and Brick stand, and I say to Kelly, "We'll be in the kitchen talking. You're safe now. You're home."

She lets out a sob, and I rush to her side, handing her a tissue. She blows her nose and looks up at me through teary eyes. "My feet hurt and my toes are tingling."

I turn to the agents. "Did a doctor exam her for injuries?"

Brick shakes his head. "The EMTs were busy with her grandfather, and we wanted to bring her home, so she could recover."

McNalley says, "It'd be a good idea to take her in for an exam. It looks like her feet took the brunt of it."

Kelly's lower lip quivers. "Granddad had a heart attack, and they took him away in an ambulance."

McNalley nods, crossing her arms.

I tilt my head. "Where is he now?"

McNalley says, "Medics transported him to a hospital in Centralia."

I frown, imagining my father being treated kindly and fawned on by medical staff. "Did they lock him up in handcuffs?"

"Yes," McNalley says, "standard procedure."

I point at McNalley and Brick and say in a hoarse voice, "He needs to be sent back to prison for the rest of his life and never see the light of day after what he did."

My cell rings, and I pull it out of my pocket out of habit. Kelly groans. "Answer it, Mom, but don't say yes to the Coast Guard. Stay home with me."

"I will, sweet girl." I answer my phone and a woman says, "Is this Irena Pickle?"

"Yes," I glance at Kelly and the agents, who are listening with concern. "That was my maiden name."

"I'm calling from the hospital in Centralia. He'd like to have a word with you."

I grip the phone with a sweaty hand, and my heart pounds. I say, "I hope you have him locked up, because he's a repeat offender and hardened criminal. He took my daughter. He was going to disappear with her."

"He'd like to have a word with you. Hold on."

Kelly's eyes brim over with tears, and I say in a firm voice, "I don't care what he wants. I have no interest in speaking with him ever again. I'm going to hang up."

My father says in a deep, gravelly voice, "Please don't. This won't take long."

I roll my eyes and stare at the ceiling. Something in the tone of his voice holds me in this spot, locked between hate and childhood love, and I wait for what he'll say next.

"Reenie, I'm sorry for what happened with Kelly. I lost my head. I've been lonely and wanted some company. Remember how we'd talk about living in a shack by a river and fishing for food? I was carrying out our dream. My health is failing, and I want you to come be by my side in my final hours."

My jaw tenses, and I shake my head. "The fishing cabin was your dream, not Mom's or mine. You're a horrible person. Don't call me again." He starts to say something, but I hang up on him.

Silence fills the room, and I say to Kelly and the FBI agents, "Don't feel sorry for him. He's a master manipulator, and he knows how to apologize and alter the truth to get his way, if bludgeoning doesn't work. He's probably making it up."

Kelly furrows her brow. "I think he's telling the truth. He looked pasty and sick when they took him away."

McNalley and Brick nod and stare at the floor. McNalley says, "You're not going to have to worry about him. After this, he'll never get out of prison."

I say, "I'm not going to feel sorry for him. Now, we'll let you rest, Kels. See if you can get some sleep."

Kelly says in a soft voice, "Love you, Mom. I'm sorry."

Leaning down, I gently kiss her head. "Sweet girl, I'm the one who is sorry. Get some rest and know that you're safe now. Try not to think about what happened."

Kelly eyes me and snorts. "Kind of hard to do when I was just abducted."

I start to laugh but catch myself. "That's my girl."

I bite my lip when it occurs to me that my father may have done unspeakable things during the time he was with her. He may be an even more horrible person than I thought. Bile rises up in my throat.

Bending down at eye level, I take her hand in mine. "I have to ask this. Did he hurt you or physically harm you in any way? I know it's difficult to talk about, but I need to know. You can trust me and tell me the truth."

She closes her eyes, pulls her hand away from mine and turns on her side. "I don't want to talk about it anymore."

Tears prick my eyes, and I blink, slowly standing and making my way to the kitchen. My father shattered my childhood and my mother's desire for a happy marriage, and now he stole Kelly's joy. When she's better one day, I'll find him, if he's alive, and teach him a final lesson he won't forget.

Going in the kitchen, I huddle with the agents, speaking in low voices. I pull out a tissue and dab at my eyes. "She's in rough shape," I say. "Thank you for finding her and bringing her home. Would you like some coffee?

Brick cocks his head. "Thanks, but we'll get some on the way."

I study their drawn faces. "Are you sure? It'll just take a minute."

McNalley shrugs. "Sure, why not, that would be great. Thanks."

Soon, we're sitting around the kitchen table holding steaming cups of black coffee. I sip scalding coffee that burns my tongue and the back of my throat, breaking into a coughing fit. My poor daughter, blaming herself for this terrible day. "What will happen to my father?"

The agents' phones buzz at the same time, and they check them, getting up from the table. McNalley says, "We have to go."

"Wait, what's going on?"

"We've got another case back towards Seattle."

They sweep out the door into the dark, snowy, windy night, and I quietly close the door, locking it and leaning back, letting silent tears stream down my cheeks. The bubble I built around my daughter is broken, and our world will never be the same.

My phone chimes with an incoming text, and out of habit I hurry to the kitchen and check it. My new business partner, Tex, who lives on a private island, wants to talk next week about our business plan. I roll my eyes and put the phone face down on the kitchen counter. It's Christmas Eve, and I don't time for anything but Kelly.

68

DUSTY

I hear someone whispering, and I stand still, listening for anyone approaching. My pulse pounds in my ears. My hands tremble with anticipation. I'm about to uncover valuables and financial documents that will bring me freedom from the shackles of working at a low wage job. My shoulders relax when all is quiet inside the house. Outside, wind roars down the street and snow swirls past a window.

Turning on my flashlight app, I scan my father's side of the room. His bare desk is dusty. His chair is empty. My throat tightens with tears. He taught me so much in this very room. A tear slides down my cheek, and I brush it away.

I grab a tissue, blow my nose as quietly as I can, and tiptoe to my mother's side of the room. I shine the light on my mother's desk chair, where her black purse sits. Tilting my head, I wonder if she set up a trap of some sort for me. She let me in the room knowing full well her purse was here.

I glance toward the door, listening, and look around the study for a hidden video surveillance camera. Nothing seems out of place on the bookshelf. I don't see new stuffed animals or suspicious artwork on the wall.

My heart thuds as I unzip her purse, and I listen for footsteps approaching. I wipe my moist palms on my pants, take a deep breath and rummage through the contents of her purse, setting her wallet aside.

I scowl and study blank scraps of paper from the purse, illuminated by the phone's flashlight. I shake my head. She got me, and she got me good. I half-smile, because this is the kind of practical joke my dad would have enjoyed. Well done, Mom. Points to you.

Opening her wallet, my mouth falls open when I see it's empty. She's been on to me from the beginning, from when I arrived at her door. That's why she let me in this off-limits room.

A manilla file folder labelled 'Financial information' rests on her desk, and I smile, picking it up. I flip it open, but there's nothing inside. I nod. Well played, Mom. You're a mighty adversary. You set me up, and I fell for it.

I glance up at the ceiling vent, rub my right cheek and remind myself that I have one final task to follow through on. I won't rest until I see what she hid in the ceiling. I shine the light on the vent and pull a screwdriver from my pocket.

I remove the last stubborn screw, and the vent starts to fall out, but I catch it and set it on the chair. I stand still as a statue and listen, but no one is coming. Smiling to myself because my search is almost over, I stick my hand up into the vent, feeling around. The duct takes a turn, and I shove my hand in deeper.

Something metal snaps down on my hand, and I yelp and jump back. A mouse trap clamped onto my fingers. I jump on one foot, shake my hand in the air and grit my teeth, so I won't yell. If I howl in pain like I'd like to, my mother will arrive and gloat over her winning a weird scavenger hunt.

Sweat beads on my brow, and I pry the offending mouse trap from my fingers. It takes all my will power not to scream and throw it across the room.

As I set the mouse trap down on her desk, my phone dies and the light blinks off, putting me in the dark. I frown and concoct a plan. I'll end her days while she's in her own bed, the way she's always wanted it. I'll smother her with a pillow. No one will be the wiser. I'll be the innocent guest sleeping on the study floor when they wake me in the morning with the sad news that Mom passed away in her sleep.

The door creaks open, and I turn. Sweat drips down my spine, despite a chill in the room.

"Uncle Dusty," Max says. "What're you doing?"

Buddy trots up to me, sniffing my hands and the mouse trap.

Mom strides in. "Yes, what're you up to?"

Mercury and Dell and Bernice and Mary and Fred and my sister Rose barge into the small room. Rose folds her arms. She shines a flashlight on Mom's unzipped purse, the open wallet, the empty folder and the missing ceiling vent.

Rose says in her older sister voice, "Shame on you, Dusty. You know better."

I shrug. "I was just bored is all. Everyone was sleeping. Nothing's going on."

Mom rolls her eyes. "I'll believe that when the sun sets in the morning. Now back to bed, all of you, and Dusty, you'll be in the dining room on the floor, unless you'd like to sleep in your truck until the snowplow comes by."

I blow out a defeated breath. "Fine. I'll go in the dining room, where I'll be cold on the bare hardwood floor. Don't worry about my bad back."

Mercury murmurs, "He knows how to spin a tale in his favor, doesn't he?"

I shuffle out of the room, and Mom locks the study behind me. She points down the hall. "Go on now. I don't want to find you anywhere near my bedroom when I'm sleeping. Not tonight and not ever. I won't trust you again."

Rose, Bernice, Mary and Fred say in unison, "Not after Shore Lodge."

"Fine," I say, brushing past them. "But Dad understood and supported me."

Mom lets out a weary sigh. "That argument is as dead as a rose bush during a drought. Better let that one go and move on with your life."

The others clap, and my face blazes with heat.

Going in the kitchen, I turn on the tap, fill a glass with water and gulp it down, staring at the snow-covered yard, where I played as a child. She's done it again and crushed my dreams. She'll regret humiliating me in front of others. I'll figure out how to get her back. Dad silenced her cutting remarks, but it's up to me now.

A smile spreads across my face. I'll get my company back. She's smart, but she doesn't know the building business like I do. I'll wait a few weeks until this dark episode is forgotten. When her defenses are down, I'll strike. Watch out, Mom, I'm coming for you.

69

JACKLYN

I stand in the living room and cross my arms, monitoring Dusty as he shuffles into the dining room. He slumps into a chair, puts his feet up on another one and lets out a loud groan. The wood chair creaks under his weight. I purse my lips and keep my comments to myself. I want this night to be over, so Dusty can go back to whatever hole in the ground he crawled from. A good mother wouldn't think like that, but I'm well beyond civilities with my devious offspring. I've. Had. Enough.

When all is quiet, I make my way to my bedroom with Buddy at my heels. Shush, shush, my slippers slap across the floor. I pull back the covers and slide into bed, still fully clothed with a wool hat on my head and socks on my feet.

I whisper to Buddy, curled up on the floor in his dog

bed, "Goodnight, sweet pup. Everything will work out fine. Sleep well."

I close my eyes and sleep, but my eyes flick open at the sound of heavy footsteps coming down the hall. The bathroom door closes, and I frown as a stream of worries flit through my mind. I know how to run a profitable garden store and assumed those skills would transfer over to running a construction company. But what if Dusty is right, and I'm wrong? Maybe I'm in over my head. Suppliers might take advantage of my being green and charge me more. Am I foolish to forge ahead and start fresh?

The bathroom door creaks opens, and someone plods down the hall to the living room. Buddy sighs in his sleep, and the sound soothes me. I adjust my head on the pillow and nod to myself. I survived my time at Shore Lodge, and I'll succeed in my new venture.

I roll over on my side, turning toward my beloved dog, and mutter to myself, "I'll build those homes in Stone Estates. Nothing's going to stop me, not even my son."

Buddy smacks his lips in his sleep, and I whisper, "It's blue skies from now on, sweet pup. We're the unbeatable team."

70

JACKLYN

The next thing I know, birds are chirping outside. I open my eyes and look around the bedroom. Buddy stretches and hops on the bed, licking my cheek, and I pat his back. Sunlight filters through the window blinds. "Fine, I'll get up."

It's cold enough in the house that I can see my breath. I swing my legs over the side and look out through the window. Thick blankets of bright white snow cover everything. I chuckle, thinking of Mary, who might say that it would be an easy scene to paint, where it's all white.

I hurry down the hall, glance at slumbering friends and family and scoop up a cup of kibble, dropping it gently into Buddy's dog bowl, so as not to wake the others. Out of habit, I flick on the lights but nothing happens. I shake my head and reach for the coffee maker but stop midmotion. No need to do that. The power is out.

My son stumbles into the kitchen, rubbing his eyes. "Coffee ready?"

I shake my head and vow to be kind enough to melt his hard heart and help him begin a new life. "Not yet. I'll have to make it on the camp stove outside."

I go over to him, and despite my qualms and fears from his devious deeds last night, I open my arms and give him a hug. He stands stiff at first, and then he melts, wrapping his arms around me. I soak in the moment, because I know this won't last.

I step back and say in a low voice, "This is a warning. We need firm boundaries from now on between us. And if only one of us can survive in this business and win, it's going to be me."

He blinks, hands hanging at his sides, and stands there a moment, gazing outside. He turns and goes in the dining room, sitting down and tugging on his work boots.

He gets up and says to me in a low voice, "See you in a bit. I'm going outside for a smoke and to check on the neighbor next-door. I'll be back."

He goes out, and Buddy runs after him, leaping through the snow. Cold air rushes inside, and I close the door. I'm tempted to lock it, but he'll find a way to worm his way into my life and my house. I know I've survived worse.

Del stands and stretches. Mercury groans. Bernice says in a bright voice, "Good morning, campers."

"Morning," Mary says, standing and yawning.

Fred stumbles off to the bathroom. Rose and Max must still be asleep.

I smile at my friends and found family. "I'm going outside to make coffee on a camp stove."

"And hot water for me," Mary says.

I knock on my son's old bedroom door and tiptoe in, taking the camp stove out of the closet. Just as I reach the door, Rose sits up. "What're you doing?"

"Getting ready to make coffee on the camp stove."

She smiles, holding up her phone. "The power just came back on. My phone is charging."

I set the camping stove back in the closet and whisper to her, so Max won't wake up, "Let him sleep as long as he can. I'll get the coffee going."

By the time I round the corner into the kitchen, everyone is gathered around laughing and cracking jokes about what we went through. The lights are on. Mercury has coffee brewing, and Mary is at the stove cooking scrambled eggs.

Someone pounds on the front door, and Del opens it. My son stomps inside carrying an armload of firewood. His boots leave a wet trail of snow on my rug, but I don't care. A bit of moisture doesn't matter today. He and I have bigger things to deal with.

He drops the load of chopped firewood that I bought and my nervy neighbor took by the fireplace and turns to grin at me. But his smile is forced, and his dark brown eyes are flat, radiating a hint of malice with an undertone of greed. We lock eyes.

The heater clicks on with a loud whine, filling the silence stretching between us, and air blows out of heating vents. We issue a collective sigh.

Dusty nods to me and shrugs. "I might as well make a fire. We're stuck here until the snowplow shows up."

"Excellent idea," I say. "I'll go help in the kitchen."

I turn and stop in my tracks, looking back. For just a flash, I thought I saw him give me the middle finger when no one was looking. I shake my head and know that although I came out on top in our minor skirmish that happened last night, our battle isn't over.

71

JACKLYN

In the kitchen, Mary serves scrambled eggs on plates and Fred adds toast. I open the refrigerator and take out jam and a butter substitute, since we're all obsessed with our health these days. Mary sidles up to me. "Everything okay? Seems so tense between you and Dusty this morning."

I nod. "Indeed it is. You could cut it with a knife, and I think it's going to be that way for a long time, unfortunately, until I prove myself and get those homes built on the hill overlooking town."

Dusty brushes past me and pours himself a cup of coffee. I inhale the rich, nutty aroma and pull out a mug.

"Coffee, Mom?" he says, looking me right in the eye.

I force myself to act casual, as if he didn't just rummage through my things, and say, "Sure, thanks."

He hands me a cup and raises the brown ceramic mug

that was his father's favorite. "Cheers, Mom," he says, studying me. "May the best person win. I'm the one who should be running Stone Construction, not you. Dad would've wanted it that way."

I arch my eyebrows. "You're not getting away with pulling a dear dad act this time. Your father's been gone for almost a year. It's time we both moved on and started new lives."

He sips his coffee, leaning against the counter. "Stone Construction is my company. I started it."

I drink coffee and it slides down my throat, waking every sleepy nerve in my body. "And it was failing until I took it over. It was losing money. If you hadn't tried to imprison me at Shore Lodge, it would still be your company."

Fred joins us. "That's right, and the company is hers now."

Dusty eyes us. "We'll see how that turns out. You may have regrets."

Goosebumps prick my arms, but I plaster a smile on my face, staring him down. I point an index finger at him. "Don't you dare try to sabotage me. I'm on to you."

"Breakfast is ready," Mary says. "Come and get it."

Dusty stands sipping coffee, staring at me and not moving.

Buddy scratches at the door, and I stride over, letting him inside and rubbing him down with a towel. I grab a plate and join the others in the dining room. Glancing around the table, I take comfort in the circle of friends and family, even if there's a clinker in the group who is my son. I know I'll have challenges in the months ahead, but I'm determined to come out on the other side.

Dusty gets up, bringing me my coffee. He sets it down and says, "Thought you'd like that with your breakfast."

I look him in the eye. "Well, thanks, hon, I appreciate that."

He claps me on the back just a little too hard, and I cough.

The next few months will be a trial, with my enemy close at hand.

We eat scrambled eggs with cheddar cheese and leftovers from last night, laughing about our crazy adventure when the power went out, a story I'm sure we'll tell for many years.

Max says, "I liked all the candles. Can we do that again next Christmas Eve?"

I chuckle. "I don't think there will be another Christmas Eve like that one, but sure, we can light as many candles as you like and make it magical."

Del speaks up. "I liked the chunks of bread dipped in chocolate for dessert."

Dusty swallows and wipes his mouth on a piece of paper towel we're using for napkins. "That's my favorite part too. Who needs the apple and banana slices? I don't."

Rose chimes in. "I do. I like those the best."

Mercury grins and tugs on the elastic strap of his party

hat. "The party hats are the best part. I wouldn't miss this next year for the world."

Bernice looks around the table and pauses when she gets to Dusty, but her gaze slides past him, and she says, "Next year, we'll all get together again right here, don't you think?"

Max grins. "With a giant sleep over and a special breakfast."

"Yes," we all say in unison.

Buddy rubs his head against my leg, and I pet his soft furry ears.

The snow plow hums, churning through heavy snow, making its way past our house. Everyone claps and cheers.

Fred sets down his napkin and stands. "We're free. We can go home."

Mary shakes a finger at him. "Not yet. Not until we do the dishes. We can't leave Jacklyn with a mess."

"Thanks," I say, "but I can handle it."

Rose gives me a look. "You don't have to do everything yourself. Accept the help."

Mary nods. "That's what I keep telling her."

Dusty says, "Me too. Accept the help. Listen to the experts."

I bristle at his last remark, gulp down a last sip of coffee and get up from the table. "Thanks, everyone. I gratefully accept your help, and then it'll be time for you to leave me to my quiet bungalow in peace, with my new friend and the best dog that ever lived."

Mercury frowns. "I offered Del a place to stay, so I need to take him there and show him around."

I smile and sigh. "It'll be a nice quiet day then, all to myself."

Dusty leans over and says to me, "Why don't I hang around and we can go over the plans Dad and I made for Stone Estates? You can pay me by the hour as a consultant."

I blow out a breath, not sure I want to be linked in any way with him or let him be involved in my business. He's clearly proven he's only out for himself. "Let me think it over," I say. "It's been a long day and night, and I could use a rest."

He looks down and blinks, and a twang of guilt plucks at my heart. But I won't be pulled in and manipulated again. I say, "Let's do the dishes, and you can get on with your lives. And Merry Christmas, everyone!"

"Merry Christmas!" The kitchen is filled with the din of happy voices, young and old. Laughter bubbles up, and dishes are washed and dried and put away, or stuck in the dishwasher. Finally, the dining table is cleared, the kitchen counters are clean, and Bernice says, "Group hug."

I groan and put a hand to my forehead. "Please, save me from this nonsense."

But Bernice gathers me in her arms and swings me around. "Come on, don't be a spoilsport. Albert would love this. Come on everyone, gather around, team hug."

Packed in with dear ones and my obstinate thieving son, we cluster together in the kitchen, touching shoulders, arms around waists and swaying side to side.

Bernice says, "Put your hands in the middle, and on the count of three, put them in the air."

We follow her orders, and I reach out, touching hands with these lovely people. My gaze catches on Mercury, and we exchange a smile. But then my eyes snag on my son's. Dusty nods to me and mouths the words, "It's not over."

Bernice says in a loud voice, "One, two, three!"

We raise our hands and cheer. We sound carefree, but deep within my bones, I know trouble lies ahead, and I'll need all my strength to wade through the coming trials and tribulations of dealing with my son and learning how to build a subdivision. But I won't back down.

Rose starts to gather her things, and I go over to her, resting a hand on her shoulder. "I didn't mean you and Max had to go. Just the others."

She drops her scarf and coat and shoves her hands in her jeans pockets. "Oh good. I'd rather not drive back today. We can stay another day."

"What about me," Dusty says, looking hurt. "You didn't ask me to stay."

I pat his shoulder. "You're welcome to join us, but I don't trust you enough to spend time alone with you in my house. Things will never be the same between us."

Max trots in the room with Buddy by his side, and he says in a loud voice, "What do you mean?"

Rose puts a finger to her lips. "Inside voice."

Max says, "Why won't things be the same?"

I lean down and say, "Shore Lodge is why."

Max nods. "That makes sense. I didn't like that place either."

Dusty frowns and rubs his flushed right cheek, which is never a good sign.

To change the subject, I say, "I wish we could play a game of croquet, but with the snow, that's out."

"Let's make snowmen," Max says.

The furnace pumps out hot air, the house is warm, and it would be good to get outside for fresh air and forget about my problems with Dusty.

"Sure," I say, "why not. I'll make a snow woman and show you how it's done."

We grab our coats, except for Buddy who is already wearing his, and race outside into the dazzling sunny day, jumping into deep snow and laughing together, forgetting our cares for one brief moment in time, until the next storm blows in.

72

ROSE

We're out playing in the snow when I glance at my brother, who is staring up at a snow-covered fir tree and mumbling to himself. I make a snowball and sneak up on him, ready to smack him and surprise him, like when we were kids. But I stop to listen to what he's saying to himself.

"Writ this in stone," he says, "and remember this deep. The bottle behind the fourth tree on the right may contain gold."

I grin and throw the snowball, aiming at his neck.

Dusty turns and blinks hard, as if I caught him in another world. But seconds later, he's back to his old self, smiling and gathering snow, forming a snowball that comes my way. I duck, but not quick enough, and it hits my face.

"Hey," I say, 'Are you okay? I heard you say something strange just now."

He shrugs. "Just a poem. It came to me, and I had to stop and listen to it."

Max runs over. "Tell me, I want to hear it."

Dusty grabs my son, tossing him in the snow, and they laugh. My brother glances at Mom, who is making snow angels and singing to herself, and he says, "Nah. Poems are private. You'll have to write your own."

He stops talking when I throw a snowball right at his face. Tears spring to his eyes, which is unusual. "Not my right cheek again," he says, but he grins and comes at me with his arms outstretched. "The snowman is coming for you, watch out."

Max giggles and trots behind Dusty. Buddy bounds in the snow, barking. I race away, laughing. Deep down, I know my brother wouldn't hurt a fly. He's got his head wrapped around getting more money since Dad died, and he needs to let it go and move on.

I trip, falling face-first in the snow, and jump up, snow stinging my cheeks. Max and Dusty pelt me with snow balls, and I laugh, returning fire. I stop for a moment, panting for breath, and a snow ball smacks my head. I grin at Mom, who has joined the enemy forces, blue eyes blazing with a snow ball in her hand, and wish we could stay frozen in this moment forever.

73

KELLY

I close my eyes and pretend to sleep on the living room couch. I'm relieved to be home safe and when I said it was my fault, I meant it with all my heart. Mom and I have always been honest with each other, but this is an exception. She can't learn the truth.

I told Granddad I wanted to run away. I was angry with Mom because she always puts her work and friends ahead of me. Her going out on her boat with friends on Christmas Eve snapped something inside, putting me in second place again.

She always rushes to rescue others, leaving me alone in the house. I was fed up and wanted to teach her a lesson. But then things turned bad when Granddad headed for Canada and wouldn't let me out of the car. He turned the ugly shade of mean that Mom mentioned to me, but I didn't believe her.

A tear trickles down my cheek, but I don't bother to brush it away. I'm ashamed of what I've done and how I brought this disaster on myself. Guilt will eat away at my insides, but Mom must never know I wanted to run away.

Thank you for reading *The Cold Night*! Please let other readers know what to expect by posting ratings and reviews on Goodreads, Amazon and BookBub.

Next up will be Book 3 in the Jacklyn Stone series.

Sign up on my website www.susanspechtoram.com for my author newsletter to hear about new releases and bookish news.

Follow me on BookBub for updates: https://www.bookbub.com/authors/susan-specht-oram

My Facebook author page is Susan Specht Oram Author

Check out my YouTube channel to see the setting for my novels @susanspechtoramauthor.

Thank you for reading my books!

ABOUT THE AUTHOR

Susan is writing mysteries-thrillers with high stakes and heart set in a fictional small Pacific Northwest town. Previously, she served as senior director of corporate communications for biotechnology companies. Susan worked as an activity aide in an upscale nursing home's secure psychiatric unit. She was a potter and painter with an art studio in Seattle and has also worked as a market researcher, a nurse's aide, a waitress, and a library page. Her essays have been published in Mothering Magazine, Twins Magazine and Utne Reader.

Susan grew up near Detroit, Michigan and received a BFA with Honors from University of Oregon and a MBA from Seattle University. She lives in a windy part of the Pacific Northwest with her husband and their rescue dog.

BOOKS BY SUSAN SPECHT ORAM

Shore Lodge

The Thieves

Cabin Eight

Secrets at the Café

The Mother's Threat

Under Jackson Bridge

Missing Man

By Midnight

The Winter Storm

The Cold Night

Humorous fiction:

Boating with Buddy, a report from a canine correspondent

Nonfiction:

Brief business books on investor relations, crisis communication and public relations

www.ingramcontent.com/pod-product-compliance
Lightning Source LLC
Chambersburg PA
CBHW071548110726
47908CB00007B/2039